SWEET SNOW

A novel
of the Ukrainian famine of 1933

Alexander J. Motyl

Červená Barva Press
Somerville, Massachusetts

Červená Barva Press
P.O. Box 440357
W. Somerville, MA 02144-3222

www.cervenabarvapress.com

Bookstore: www.thelostbookshelf.com

Cover Photograph: Mark Hewko

Cover Design: William J. Kelle

ISBN: 978-0-9883713-7-8

Library of Congress Control Number: 2013936882

Distributed by Small Press Distribution: www.spdbooks.org

To Michael Bojczuk and Bohdan Hevko,

the uncles I never knew.

SWEET SNOW

A novel
of the Ukrainian famine of 1933

The black rat darted behind the shit bucket as the heavy iron gate creaked open. A diminutive man in an absurdly large brown coat stumbled inside. He was panting, laboriously and irregularly, like an asthmatic who had just climbed five flights of steep stairs. As the gate slammed shut and two pairs of footsteps receded arhythmically along the dimly lit corridor to the right, the man extended his left arm and unintentionally brushed his fingers against the rough concrete wall. He drew back and leaned over to catch his breath, inhaling and exhaling purposefully, almost as if he were readying himself for another climb. Drops of warm sweat trickled down his forehead, bypassing his thick eyebrows, and made their way down his bulbous nose. He wiped them away with the back of his right hand, rubbed his moist brow, and adjusted his metal-rimmed glasses. The left lens was cracked. He coughed and felt a thick knot of foul-tasting phlegm rising to his throat. As he spat into the bucket, the rat scurried alongside the wall and hid beneath the heavy wooden bench at the man's feet.

The man felt a stabbing pain in his right lung and winced. He placed the fingers of his right hand on the spot, just below the collarbone, drank in the cold air, and waited for the pain to subside. His eyes pressed shut, his mouth just slightly open, and the tip of his parched tongue protruding between his teeth, he rotated his head, almost touching his chest with his chin, and listened to the gentle crackling in his tense neck. It was reassuring to hear oneself, to be reminded that one was still in possession of a firm body that contained bones and sinews and muscles and could move and make sounds despite the abuse it had endured. It was reassuring to be alive, even if just barely. As the stench of the bucket rose to his nostrils, he jerked his head to the left with disgust and coughed, repeatedly and uncontrollably, loudly clearing his throat and depositing globs of mucus into the filthy receptacle.

Golub ran his right sleeve across his brow, leaving an elongated smudge on his forehead, just below his thick, black hair. He dropped his hand to his side and stood as straight as he could, tilting his head back until his nose pointed at the ceiling. The cold air was both exhilarating and enervating. He ran both hands along the sides of his greatcoat. The belt was missing and the long slit in the back exposed navy blue pants and an oily stain running down both legs. His thin-soled black shoes, their laces gone, peered out from beneath the scuffed rim of the coat. He undid the to

3

buttons of the coat and extended his chin, turning carefully to face the gate and, with palms held parallel to the ground, sliding onto the bench with a prolonged groan. The rat returned to its place behind the shit bucket, but the man heard nothing, concentrating on the cold hard wood of the bench and the claustrophobic chamber in which he happened to be sitting.

The cell was about two yards by three. The bench stood along the longer wall and the dented metal bucket occupied the corner to its left. The floor was moist, with shimmering puddles collecting randomly in the indentations; so, too, were the walls, adorned with mostly indecipherable signs, words, and squiggles scratched into the concrete, once presumably a light gray and now a dark charcoal punctuated by the unevenly spaced shadows left by the greasy hair and dirty necks of the cell's many miserable inhabitants. The irony was inescapable: the inmates' faint traces probably went back decades, to pre-revolutionary times, when the prisoners were most likely the ideological predecessors of his jailers.

To Golub's left, some four yards from the ground, a small window served as the only source of air. It was just large enough to accommodate a woman's thigh, but much too small for anyone to entertain thoughts of escape. When he leaned forward and turned his eyes upward and to the left, Golub could glimpse a patch of sickly white sky slashed in two by a vertical iron bar. A gust of frigid air blew into the cell and he realized that he was terribly cold. His teeth had begun chattering and he drew the coat tightly around his chest. He coughed and tried to assuage the pain in his lung by rubbing the spot and taking shallow breaths. His stomach moaned uneasily and he recalled that he had not eaten since his arrest several days ago. Just how many he couldn't say, as he had lost all track of time during the seemingly endless interrogation that had merged all colors, sensations, and feelings into a viscous pulp.

*

They had come one or two hours after midnight—just as he had finally settled into a deep slumber—had given him five minutes to dress, and had escorted him by his quivering elbows down the carpeted staircase, across the empty hotel lobby that smelled of cheap cigarettes and sour sweat, past the somnolent night clerk pretending to be busy with dog-eared files, and out the front door to the waiting black car, its side windows covered with frost, its motor purring, its windshield wipers squeaking. He had protested, he had asked for an explanation, he had shown them his Party credentials and letters of referral, but they had said nothing, almost as if they knew that their very presence said all there was to say. It was their bored, mechanical, and indifferent silence that had most intimidated him.

He was pushed into the lumpy back seat, where he sat, stunned, between two silent agents, with only the clothes on his back and without the little suitcase with essentials—socks, underwear, scarf, toothbrush—that enemies of the people fearful of the midnight knock usually left lying near the door. After reaching their destination, a bleak structure with opaque grated windows and unevenly shaped columns on both sides of the grandiose entrance, they shoved him out the vehicle, through the door, down the corridors, and up the stairs, into an oppressively small interrogation room—painted black or olive green: he couldn't tell which—with an uncomfortable, straight-backed metal chair bolted to the floor, for him, and a metal table and wooden chair, for the interrogator, and a piercingly bright lamp suspended from the ceiling on a thick cord just above his head.

Then the silence abruptly ended and the stone-faced interrogator spoke incessantly, repeating the same questions over and over—sometimes kindly, sometimes impatiently, sometimes savagely, always monotonously—listening to the same answers, rejecting them again and again as outrageous lies and impudent attempts to evade the people's righteous wrath, and admonishing Golub to tell the truth because it was his duty to tell the truth, because the Party insisted that he tell the truth, because *their* people always told the truth, because telling the truth was for the good of the revolution, and because he had no choice but to tell the truth that the Party defined as the truth anyway.

He told the truth that they wanted to hear and then at some point he realized that he no longer knew what the truth was, that there might even be no such thing as the truth—except of course that he was and would always remain a communist, that Stalin was a genius, that the Soviet Union was a workers' state, that the dusty stoops of New York's Orchard Street were his home, that Babe Ruth and Lou Gehrig were the best hitters on the Yankees' Murderers Row, and that Katz's served the best pastrami in town. At some later point—perhaps a minute later, possibly a day later—they unbound him from the bolted metal chair, gave him a dead man's greatcoat, and brought him to the cell. What would happen next? Would the questions continue? Would they beat him? Would they believe him? Would they finally realize they had made a terrible mistake and release him?

The aperture had turned the color of a motley wolf. The wind whistled fitfully outside and occasional snowflakes dashed into the room, usually accompanied by howling gusts of freezing air. Golub's sallow eyes scoured the cell for a toilet and, when they came to rest on the bucket whose silhouette was just visible in the half-darkness to his left, he felt foolish, even embarrassed. He extended his sodden legs and carefully rotated his feet, first to the left, then to the right. The shoes, at least one size too small, weren't his. He no longer remembered when and why they had confiscated the thick-soled, practical American shoes with sturdy shoelaces he had bought on Delancey and given him these, presumably a dead man's as well.

He planted both feet on the concrete floor and pushed himself up, his wrists aching, his shoulders sore, his eyes heavy with sleep that would not come. After he stumbled toward the bucket, Golub fumbled with the buttons on his trousers. He felt a searing pain. Something was wrong. He looked down and saw that his right pant leg and coat flap were wet. The comparison was absurd, of course, but he felt like a Bowery bum, the kind who'd just been on a binge, had been rolled by some toughs, and lay in an alley, his legs splayed, his trousers torn, and the urine trickling down the cracked sidewalk, from his wet crotch to the trash-filled gutter. Compared to this cell, the flophouses and gin mills beneath the elevated train that rumbled up and down the Bowery and Third Avenue were palatial. And the bums, despite the awful squalor of their lives, still had their liquor. Besides, no one had dragged them out of bed at two in the morning, subjected them to the hammering of a faceless accuser, and deposited them unceremoniously in an ice box.

It was pitch black in the cell now and Golub, trembling violently from the cold and wishing for a double shot of whiskey and a greasy ham sandwich, crawled onto the bench, brought his knees to his chin, and sank his head into the coat. He began exhaling deeply. The warmth of his breath calmed his beating heart and, although a piercingly loud siren went off outside, he was soon snoring. The rat peered out from behind the bucket and made its way to the sleeping man. It raised its head, sniffed the air, and returned to the safety of its hiding place.

*

The discordant jangling of heavy keys followed by the familiar creaking of the gate jarred Golub into consciousness. As he lowered the greatcoat beneath his bloodshot eyes and raised himself a few inches off the bench, he caught sight of a distinguished-looking man, at least six feet in height, wearing a sleek black leather coat and standing uncertainly before him. His short white hair glowed like phosphorous and he had the kind of square jaw that mugs and cops had in the funnies, the kind of long, thin nose one associated with Park Avenue Protestant severity, and the kind of thick, jet-black Prussian mustache with upturned ends that adorned anti-Hun posters during the war. He struck Golub as someone who had mysteriously been propelled, with the assistance of an infernal Wellsian time machine, half a century into the future. Despite his imposing appearance, he was shaking, possibly from fright, possibly from exhaustion and cold, and shuffling his feet gracefully, almost as if he were doing a jig. His cuffed brown woolen pants retained traces of having once been neatly pressed and his light brown shoes had thin leather soles and tassels. To Golub's surprise, he wore no socks: he was obviously no policeman come to finish the interrogation.

The man turned toward the gate and seized the iron bars with his smooth hands. Instead of rattling them, however, he stood quietly, motionlessly, neither moaning, nor shouting. Then, after a brief period of Stoic composure, he unexpectedly bent over and grabbed his stomach with both hands. A long, low growl crawled out of his gut. As the man cast desperate looks around the cell, Golub pointed to the bucket in the corner. The man rushed toward it, lifted his trousers to prevent buckling at the knees, fell forward, and, almost in the manner of a devout pilgrim approaching an altar, dropped his head and let loose an anguished cry. The sour smell of vomit reached Golub's nostrils and he hid his head inside his coat until the retching was over.

"*Danke,*" he heard the man say.

The newcomer placed his left hand on the edge of the

bench and raised himself hesitantly to his feet. He stood unsteadily, swaying very slightly, almost as if he were tipsy, the fingers of both hands pressed against his temples and eyes. He then turned to Golub, blinked and squinted, twirled one end of his mustache, and, after making a weak effort at clicking his heels, introduced himself.

"August Graf"—he gulped awkwardly—"von Mecklenburg." The man stood ramrod straight and appeared to study Golub.

Golub returned the stare.

"Sol Golub"—a wrinkle crossed his lips—"*Kommunist aus New York.*"

He had no reason to declare his political leanings, but he couldn't resist waving the red flag before the aristocracy he detested with every fiber of his being, and especially before one of its pompous, war-mongering, Prussian representatives. The German's response came as no surprise.

"*Jude?*" The man raised one black eyebrow.

"I have heard that there are many Jews in New York City." He fixed his stern gaze on Golub's long face.

"I have been told that America is the land of boundless opportunity, where the streets are paved with gold and every boy can become president. My friends have been there and they assure me that Europe is on the verge of extinction and that the celebrated Yankee know-how will soon rule the world. Personally, I have no particular opinions on this issue, nor do I care much about the future of America, all the more so as I have never—"

"They are all refugees from anti-Semitism." Golub cleared his throat and, self-consciously mimicking the burly sailors who congregated near the East River's docks, sent a thick clam in the direction of the bucket.

"*German* anti-Semitism."

Von Mecklenburg turned away, drawing his thin, long, pianist's fingers through his hair. He brushed his hands against his coat and crossed his arms in the manner of a judge about to deliver an unpleasant verdict. After peering at the aperture, he took a step toward the bench. As Golub hurriedly withdrew his legs and sat upright in the corner, the German planted himself carefully on its unyielding surface.

"*Kalt,*" he exclaimed softly, seemingly in response to the flurry of snowflakes that fell upon him, "*so verdammt kalt.*"

The German withdrew his hands from his pockets and rubbed them vigorously. He cupped them around his nose and mouth and sucked in the air hungrily. The tips of his mustache vibrated. He removed his right shoe, placed it beneath his right thigh, and began rubbing his foot. A few minutes later, he performed the same procedure on his left shoe and left foot. The soles of his feet were bruised, creating a striking contrast to his toenails, which were as neatly rounded as his fingernails. After deftly slipping the shoes on his feet, he leaned back against the concrete wall and extended both legs. Then he raised his coat collar, folded his arms over his chest, and, after blinking nervously, exhaled loudly and shut his eyes.

Golub draped the coat over his head and feet and embraced his knees. The window shimmered with twilight.

*

The gate swung open with a long squeal. Both men opened their eyes and espied a short blond man with a round face, large darting eyes, and bright red cheeks. His hands fastened to the metal bars on both sides of the gate, his head thrown back in melodramatic fashion, and his small feet pressed stubbornly against the floor, he stood his ground as two thick-set guards, eyes bulging and nostrils flaring above thick woolen coats, were shoving him inside. All three grunted, but none spoke. It was, thought the German, like watching the exaggerated expressions in a pantomime or a film, perhaps a scene from Caligari. Only the heavy make-up, the Expressionist set, and the piano accompaniment were missing. The shorter guard with a stubby nose and assertive chin withdrew a shiny night stick from his belt and poked it fiercely into the man's side. As he let go of the bars, the other guard delivered a swift kick to his backside. The little man extended his hands to break the fall, but the force of the blow sent him sprawling to the floor.

"*Cholera!*" The little man let loose a string of curses: "*Kurwa, kurwa, kurwa, kurwa...*"

"*Pan jest polakiem?*" von Mecklenburg asked casually in heavily accented Polish.

"Of course," the man responded with the annoyance of someone who has to explain the obvious to a dolt. "Of course, I am a Pole—of course."

Dressed in tails, a starched white shirt, and a large bow tie, he was kneeling before the bench, eyes cast downward, rubbing his forehead and temples with both hands. His fingers were short and plump and, the count noticed with satisfaction, his nails were trimmed. The Pole was obviously a well-educated man, perhaps even a nobleman, and von Mecklenburg switched to German.

"I must confess something to you. I have always wondered why my farm workers said that—'*Kurwa.*' Why is 'whore' a swear word? Can you, or anyone for that matter, explain that to me? In Berlin, their excellent services command a high price. Indeed, I dare say some are quite charming, especially when they refrain from painting their faces and using too much powder. In Paris, they live quite elegantly and those who have the good fortune, and skills, to establish themselves as courtesans could be the envy of many a fine lady. From what I have seen in Warsaw, they are not so different in Poland." The count slid toward the middle of the bench.

"They say that it is the world's oldest profession and I dare say they must be right. About the second oldest we shall talk some other time perhaps. Longevity alone deserves respect, I should think, but, instead, we treat the word almost as badly as we treat the practitioners of this noble guild. Curious, is it not?"

Golub watched the Prussian's exaggerated performance carefully. He snorted, opened his mouth as if to respond, but then retracted his head into the thick folds of his coat. The Pole had ceased listening almost immediately after the German had launched his peroration. It was astounding, but the old man was a rhetorical *Doppelgänger* for the Lycée's most notorious academic popinjay, Professor Kowalski, a dwarf of a man who always wore a toga and had an opinion about everything but never knew when to desist from pontificating and never seemed to notice that every fatuous word he uttered reinforced his reputation as a deadly bore.

The Pole held his right hand on his forehead and pushed with his left against the concrete floor. Once standing, he realized that his trousers were torn, in a long gash extending from the back of his right leg to his crotch.

"*Kurwa!*"

"*Es macht doch nichts. Bald sind wir alle tot.*"

"*Co?*"

"It doesn't matter, he said," Golub explained from within his coat. "We will all be dead soon, he said. I'm not so sure, but that's what the Prussian said."

"*Ich weiss, ich weiss*—I know," the Pole said with a hint of exasperation, "*Ich verstehe Deutsch*—I understand." The Pole observed his two interlocutors closely.

"We appear to be a polyglot community. I take it all of us speak English as well?"

"Obviously," replied von Mecklenburg. "*Selbstverständlich.* Every German diplomat does."

"As does every *Polish* diplomat," the Pole snapped back. Then he looked in Golub's direction.

"And you, sir—in the big coat? Are you also one of us?"

"One of *you*?" Golub snickered.

"A diplomat. I mean, are you a diplomat?"

"No, a journalist." A second later, Golub added: "American."

Von Mecklenburg arched both eyebrows this time.

"An American journalist from New York City?" He spoke grandly, as if he were presiding at an official ceremony.

"It is, I believe, the city of brotherly love—is it not?— where refugees from German anti-Semitism and noble communists live in peace, harmony, and eternal brotherhood in the shadow of the Liberty Statue. And American journalism is, of course, a profession fit for philosopher kings. May we assume, Herr Journalist von New York, that your dedication to truth and honesty are unconditional? That your vocation is unsullied by ideology, power, and money?" The count paused, as if to think, before continuing with a seeming revelation.

"But wait, *mein lieber Herr!* How can you reconcile your communism with your devotion to your craft? Could it be that we are in the presence of, may the good Lord help us, a contradiction? Or," von Mecklenburg sneered, "are you just a cheap scribbler, a paid propagandist who writes whatever the Party instructs him to see"—and now came what the Pole guessed would be the *coup de grâce*—"in short, a *kurwa*? Tell us, Herr Journalist von New York. Which is it?"

"I am a Bolshevik," Golub stated firmly. "And I serve the working class."

*

A shot rang out somewhere in the building and, as if on cue, the visibly shivering Pole muttered, *"Mir ist kalt."* The count moved to the side of the bench and motioned to him to sit down.

"Asseyez-vous, s'il vous plaît. And you, Herr Journalist von New York," von Mecklenburg called to Golub, "please move closer to our Polish friend. No doubt he, too, suffers from Prussian anti-Semitism and, as you may have guessed from his shockingly non-proletarian attire, he is either an aristocrat or a bourgeois gentleman. But blue blood also freezes, I fear, just like working class blood, so please be so good as to consider moving closer— *bitte."*

As the Pole lowered himself onto the bench, the count placed his heavy arm around his slim shoulders and drew him gently to himself. Bemused, embarrassed, and curious, the scarlet-faced Pole observed von Mecklenburg out of the corner of his eyes, but said nothing.

"We will keep you warm, *mein lieber Herr.* You will not die, not just yet. As to tomorrow, *wer weiss*—who knows? Perhaps we will live, perhaps we will not. Meanwhile, you need rest. You must sleep."

The count began humming some tune and, after a few notes, stopped.

"Perhaps I can sing you to sleep, my young friend?"

The Pole remained silent.

"It is rumored that I have a passable voice, which, while unlikely ever to grace the stage at La Scala, has been known to amuse my wife and closest friends—who, I admit, may be too polite to speak the full truth. I fear I know no Polish songs and Prussian marches would, I suspect, only annoy our comrade from New York, but I think you will agree that I have the perfect tune for the occasion."

Von Mecklenburg began singing, softly and melodiously, into the Pole's ear:

> *O, du lieber Augustin, Augustin, Augustin,*
> *O, du lieber Augustin, alles ist hin.*

The Pole listened in disbelief. Was the garrulous old man purposely imitating a third-rate cabaret performer or was he blissfully unaware of his ridiculous behavior? Probably the latter, *hélas:* the German obviously lacked the capacity to see himself as he appeared to others. In any case, his body exuded warmth and the

Pole resolved not to protest. There would be enough time tomorrow, or the day after, to register his displeasure with the batty count's posturing and assert himself. For the time being, all that mattered was rest and, if he had to listen to a German folk song about death to get it, then so be it. Besides, there was something to be said for the old man's condescending attitude. It was good to be underestimated, especially under conditions of uncertainty and danger. It was even better for strangers, and potential enemies, to believe he was helpless.

Geld ist weg, Mensch ist weg,
Alles hin, Augustin.
O, du lieber Augustin,
Alles ist hin.

The Pole quickly fell asleep to the count's improvised lullaby about the end of everything. A thin shaft of light quivered between the window and the wall opposite it. The snow had stopped falling, but the insolent wind persisted in forcing its way into the cell. The three men sat huddled together, like Alpine hikers trapped in an unexpectedly sticky fog.

His back stiff and his hands folded on his lap, von Mecklenburg stared straight ahead at the gate and the narrow corridor behind it. Were it not for its color, a ghastly green that had been slapped on carelessly with a thin brush, it could have been the underground passage that led from the storeroom with the meats and pickled vegetables and fruits to the wine cellar stocked with rows of bottles that he used to take such great pleasure in dusting and turning, as if they were precious Mycenaean artifacts.

The villa and the estate were long gone, as were the passage and the wine. Who drank it all? The Russians? The Germans? The Poles? Did the wild-eyed *Soldateska* even suspect they were imbibing vintage wines, some over one hundred years old? Of course not. War dehumanized everyone and even the clean-shaven young officers who trespassed on his cellar probably guzzled his best ports as if they were some rotgut that sold for pennies in any village bazaar. He sighed. The world had changed, and not for the better, at least not for him and his kind. He had become a museum piece, a fragile statuette that required dusting twice a week. Perhaps the American's derisiveness was not wholly unjustified. He was a fourfold brute, of course—an American, a journalist, a communist, and a Jew—but even brutes could, perhaps due to their very lack of sophistication, occasionally see with lucidity.

Geld ist weg, Mensch ist weg,
Alles hin, Augustin.
O, du lieber Augustin,
Alles ist hin.

Von Mecklenburg shut his eyes. It was true: *Alles ist hin.* Everything was dead.

*

A siren cracked the frigid air and unleashed volleys of marching boots. After guttural commands were delivered in incomprehensible Russian, the boots broke into a raspy run, rusty gates were banged shut, and a deep, cold silence settled on the cell like a wet blanket. The three men were motionless, occasionally coughing, grunting, sighing, or shifting their weight from one side of their exhausted bodies to the other. The light slithered down the concrete wall, narrowed, and finally disappeared. Both men and dogs barked outside, especially when heavy footsteps scratched the snow. The wind blew through the window, sometimes whistling like a melancholy drunk, sometimes moaning like a distant train rumbling across the steppe.

Toward the evening, as the aperture turned dark, snowflakes stormed into the cell, coming to rest like moths on the German's left shoulder. Von Mecklenburg began rubbing it with his right hand.

"Herr Journalist," he said softly, "let us change places." The man in the coat failed to respond, so he spoke with greater insistence.

"Herr Journalist, can you hear me? We *must* change places."

There was silence—followed by a pithy observation. *"Sie sind Deutscher."*

The count shrugged, knowing what would come next. Golub was, like all his fourfold kind, so dreadfully predictable.

"You are a Nazi."

"Really? *Seit wann?*" Von Mecklenburg chortled, both pleased with his predictive powers and distraught at the prospect of a lengthy conversation that could only lead nowhere while he shivered.

"Since when, Herr Journalist von New York? Please enlighten me. But before you do, let us change places—*bitte*. I am freezing. *Ich friere*."

"Only Nazis wear black leather coats."

For a second von Mecklenburg was dumbstruck. He opened his mouth, but then changed his mind and snapped it shut. What could he say in response to such an assertion? What sort of Bolshevik paid attention to such irrelevant details? He turned toward the American, opened his coat, and pointed to the patch.

"A Parisian house, Herr Journalist von New York. See? You cannot because of the darkness, of course, but I can assure you that it is there. Are the French Nazis, too? *Nein*, Herr Journalist von New York, the story is much less interesting and I fear that it will bore you to tears. You see, I have money. Are you shocked? Do not be. I admire stylish clothes. Now you are surely shocked and I apologize from the bottom of my degenerate heart. And because I can afford them, I buy them. Can you imagine, Herr Journalist von New York? I *buy* them. How capitalist of me, *nicht wahr*? Indeed, how imperialist! And not a trace of the dialectic!" Weary of his own irony, the count buttoned his coat.

"And now, Herr Golub, let us change seats. *Mir ist kalt, mir ist verdammt kalt*. I am cold, and my left shoulder is quite numb. *Et voila*. So, please—*bitte*, let us change places and then we can all return to hunting phantom Nazis in our sleep."

Golub and von Mecklenburg filed past each other without saying a word. A flash of light swept across the ceiling. A dog barked with unusual ferocity and boots crunched in the snow. Someone could be heard speaking, someone else shouted, and then there was a series of shots—followed by silence, the sound of boots thumping like drums along the frozen ground, the whining of dogs, and the distant howling of what might have been wolves.

"An execution," said the German blandly. The sounds were unmistakable, as he knew all too well. No matter how many he witnessed, no matter who was shot, no matter what the circumstances, the executions never failed to touch him. To die on the battlefield was arguably heroic. To die blindfolded before a pock-marked wall made no sense at all.

"Soon it will be our turn," he announced.

"*Your* turn, Mister Mecklenburg," Golub said defiantly. "*I am innocent.*"

The Pole opened his eyes just long enough to exclaim: "You communists are as innocent as the serpent."

*

The wind's low tones underscored the seamless blackness between the inside of the cell and the night outside. The men snored, sitting perfectly still, almost as if they knew that even the smallest adjustment of their clothes or limbs would expose some errant body part to the icy cold and awaken them with a start. For a brief moment during the long night the dirge-like hum of a distant train wafted through the cell and remained suspended, like an unanswered question, in the air. Whenever screams or commands rent the stillness, the frantic barking of dogs erupted, subsiding only when equally frantic shrieks reduced them to submission. Once, a horse neighed and a whip cracked and wheels appeared to turn.

The rat emerged from behind the shit bucket, scurried beneath the bench, and approached the German's outstretched legs. It sniffed his bare ankle, hesitated as if uncertain what to do next, and clambered onto his shin. It paused before proceeding up his pant leg and coming to a halt a centimeter or two above where his knee lay exposed beneath the flap of the coat. Perhaps sensing the weight on his leg, von Mecklenburg cautiously opened his left eye. He could just barely discern the rat in the darkness. It was still, for now, and he realized that a well-placed blow with his right hand could send it flying across the cell and against the concrete wall. It was all a matter of stealth and timing—not unlike a surprise attack on an enemy outpost in the war. He recalled how the Makhno anarchists had perfected the maneuver, striking German units so suddenly and unexpectedly as if they had appeared out of, and then dissolved into, thin air, leaving behind scores of bloody bodies hacked to pieces by machine guns and curved sabers.

Jawohl, everything hinged on the element of surprise—the key to tactical and, just as often, strategic victory. Von Mecklenburg began withdrawing his hand from the coat pocket, careful not to rub leather against leather or produce the lightest tremor. As luck would have it—the count knew that what the great Machiavelli called *fortuna* was an indispensable component of every successful campaign—the rat was preoccupied with sniffing his coat and was therefore eminently vulnerable to attack. All was going exactly according to plan and in another second or two he could pounce. Alas, at that very moment *fortuna* prematurely reared its Janus-faced head and one of his cellmates let loose an exceptionally loud snort. The element of surprise was obviously lost. *Es war jetzt oder nie*—it was now or never—and von Mecklenburg struck the rat with the outstretched fingers of his hand. It squealed like a pig, tumbled through the darkness, slapped the hard wall, and fell to the floor with a thud.

"*Co to było?*" the Pole asked with a hint of alarm in his voice. "What was that?" He sat upright and looked nervously about him.

"Is someone coming? Is it the police?"

Von Mecklenburg beamed triumphantly as he stroked his mustache. It was a small victory, but a victory nonetheless, one that boded a possible turnaround in their fortunes.

"*Eine Ratte*," he answered calmly. "It is on the ground, somewhere over there, to your left. Grab it before it recovers and runs off."

"I don't understand. Why?"

"We can eat it."

"*Cholera jasna. Czy pan głupie?*"

Golub's head emerged from within his coat.

"He's not crazy," he said as he extended his legs and lowered them carefully to the ground. After patting the floor in a semi-circular motion, one foot found something soft.

"I have it." He pressed down on his heel until he heard the gut burst.

"Bravo, Herr Journalist!" von Mecklenburg cried. "*Jetzt haben wir Frühstück.*"

The Pole turned his head away in disgust.

"Breakfast? I for one will never—"

"Were you on the front, *mein lieber Herr?*" Delicate sensibilities were completely out of place in the trenches and von Mecklenburg's tone became clipped and harsh.

"I was just a boy then."

"*Moi*—three years, two near Ypres and one year here. One could say I know what the front is like—what war is like. Do you know what war is like, my young friend? Do you know what it is like to live in a trench?"

"How could I?"

"Then let me tell you, my young Polish friend. It is hell—
eine Hölle. It is something you do not want to experience, especially
not for three years. Permit me to tell you, my young Polish friend,
that you are very fortunate to be so young."

"My father told me things. He said—"

"We were always tired, always terrified, always dirty, always
smelly, always wet—and *immer hungrig.* Even officers such as I were
unable to escape the grasp of that demon whose name is hunger."

"In the army they taught us to eat insects and worms."

"In the trenches the choice before us was to eat nothing or
to learn to eat everything—*alles.*"

"Even human flesh?"

"*Nein.* After all, there are limits to—"

"But you would have!" Golub interjected excitedly. "I was
in Verdun in 1918. I saw the French and the Germans when they
crawled out of their caves and forts. They were half-human. The
imperialist war had turned them into beasts—into mindless
brutes."

"*Ach so!* Then you know."

"*Ja,*" Golub replied. "I know."

"Know what?" asked the Pole. "Know what? What are you
talking about?"

"That rats are a delicacy."

"*Matko Boska!* Mother of God!"

"Especially if raw," said Golub with a casual flick of his
hand. "Then they are fresh, uncontaminated—probably." He
picked up the rat by its tail and handed it to von Mecklenburg.

"Here, Nazi, here is your rat. Here is our breakfast."

*

The siren wailed shrilly and the three men awoke. The sun may
have risen and the opening resembled an aluminum sheet. Their
fingers, mouths, and chins were splattered with dried blood. As the
Pole rubbed his cold hands and cupped them over his mouth, he
smelled the rat's blood encrusted on his fingernails, moaned
pathetically, and retched, ejecting a thin sliver of dark bile onto his
blood-stained shirt. An indefinable odor rose to his nostrils.
Nauseous, he cried "*Matko Boska!*" and retched again.

It was hard to believe, but he had eaten a rat. He recalled the sickening sound of breaking bones and tearing skin. One of the bloody parts had found itself in his own reluctant hands. Had he really chewed the meat? Had he swallowed? It was impossible that he could have. And yet, the blood on his hands and shirt indicated that he, too, had become a barbarian, or worse—a Cossack. The sickening warmth returned to his face and he hurried to the window, sucked in the cold air, and resumed wiping his shirt.

"Where are we?" he said distractedly. "Does anyone know?"

"In the Union of Socialist Soviet Republics, of course."

"*Tak, tak*, I know," the Pole said with unconcealed irritation. "But this place—where is this place?"

"It would seem that we are in a communist jail. Is that not correct, Herr Journalist von New York?"

Golub spoke softly and his tone was as solemn as a requiem.

"It is a mistake. They made a *mistake*. And they will correct their mistake."

Von Mecklenburg was fully alert now and he smiled broadly. "Come, come, Herr Journalist, we are not in your squalid New York. In glorious Russia, in the land of the victorious proletariat, communists make no mistakes! Surely you know that. Why, even I—how did you put it, comrade?—even I, a Nazi and an anti-Semite, know that. And I wager that our sensitive young Polish friend knows it, too."

"These people—these people are not real communists. They are not true Bolshe—"

"Really?" the Pole asked, his back against the wall. "So what exactly are they if they are not real communists?"

It was, Golub realized, no accident that the Pole's counter-revolutionary question brought to mind his debates with the Union Square social fascists who had advocated abandoning the Party line. Those fruitless exchanges had taught him one thing: that the best defense, at least for a Bolshevik, was always to storm the citadels of capitalism. The decadent aristocracy lacked the stomach for sustained class warfare. Onward was the only correct proletarian response to bourgeois provocations. And it was, and had to be, onward for him—*only* onward and *always* onward.

"The people will *smash* them with a single blow. The

people will *never* tolerate—"

"The people are dying, Herr Golub," the Pole corrected him. "How can they smash anything, when *they* are being smashed?"

"It is the kulaks who are being eliminated as a class, while Stalin and the Party—"

"The Party?" the German shouted, unable to restrain himself. "Your Party is a band of criminals and your Stalin is a murderer!"

"And *you*," Golub stammered, "you *Nazis*—what are *you*? You burn books, you break windowpanes, you build prisons—and you beat Jews!"

The count rose to his feet. He hesitated for a second before replying as matter-of-factly as possible.

"That little man is vulgar, but we Germans will not tolerate—"

"*Tolerate?*" the Pole sneered. He could not tolerate another evasion by either man. It was time to set the record straight, even if that meant being indelicate.

"They voted for him," he stated definitively. "They support him. They march with him. I have seen their eyes. He is their god—their messiah." Then the Pole delivered the fatal blow: "You Germans *adore* him."

The charges were not, alas, wholly untrue and von Mecklenburg decided to reestablish his equilibrium before responding.

"As I was saying," he continued, "we Germans will not— we *cannot*—tolerate his crudeness for long. *Jawohl, meine Herren*, we will not and we cannot."

He then adopted a tone of nonchalance.

"As to your concerns, rest assured, gentlemen, that only a minority—only the frightened little people *adore*, as you put it, my young Polish friend, that little man. Thank God that we have von Hindenburg and von Papen. They are sly foxes. They will keep Herr Hitler on a short leash."

"Monopoly capitalism needs fascism," Golub shot back, "and fascism needs monopoly capitalism! Your Hitler is here to stay, Herr—"

"*Graf*," said the German, thankful for the perfect diversion. "*Count* August von Mecklenburg." He enunciated each syllable and smiled graciously.

The blaring of a truck horn interrupted the stillness that followed the count's proud proclamation and both Golub and von Mecklenburg turned their heads, inadvertently and almost imperceptibly, toward the window. The Pole had turned an even brighter crimson. It was one thing to expressly oneself directly in a debate, but how could he have failed to follow the most elementary rules of polite society and introduce himself? His *faux pas* was inexcusable, even in a prison cell, and especially in the presence of an aristocrat. He took two steps to the iron gate and, with his arms at his sides, turned toward the others.

"You must forgive my rudeness," he said with a deep bow of his head. "Zbigniew Pieracki, cultural attaché at the Polish consulate. I have no excuse for my intolerable behavior, gentlemen. Please accept my most sincere apologies."

Von Mecklenburg returned the bow, while Golub, sensing that the tide had turned decisively in his favor, pressed the attack.

"So why the hell do you think you're here, *Mister Count?*"

The sarcasm fell flat. The boorish American had lost the moral high ground and the count knew exactly how to press his advantage.

"My ill-fated presence in these surroundings is no mistake, Herr Golub von New York. Of that I am absolutely certain. Your so-called proletarian state *must* destroy us. That is why all of us are here: to be destroyed, or smashed, as you might say"—von Mecklenburg made a fist and brought it down in the palm of his hand—"*wie Fliegen*, like flies, for the simple reason that we have borne witness to its extravagant crimes.

"Have you seen the corpses? Have you seen the thousands of dead bodies littering the streets?"

"There is mass famine," added Pieracki somberly. "I have seen it with my own eyes."

"There are *difficulties* and Comrade Stalin is—"

"There is *starvation* and they are bloating up and dying in all the villages. And they come to the cities and they die there, too. Everywhere, Herr Golub, they are dying everywhere. Millions— *millions* are dying. Everyone but you and your Comrade Stalin appears to know that simple fact."

"Fascist propaganda! Fascist lies!"

Von Mecklenburg laughed, but it was a bitter, almost

forced laugh.

"Permit me to tell you something, Herr Golub. You are like our dear Führer. Yes, that is what you are, that is exactly what you and your comrades are: vulgar simpletons, ignorant and violent little boys, who have no idea just how primitive and stupid you really are." After rubbing his hands, he added: "The most you will crush is a rat."

What was he to say to the incorrigible Nazi and his Piłsudskiite underling? Golub rose from the bench and strode to the bucket, where he undid his pants and began urinating. When he was done, he stood before the aperture, to Pieracki's right, and, with his back turned demonstratively toward the count, painstakingly filled his tired lungs with icy air.

*

Energized by the skirmish that had silenced the impudent little Bolshevik, von Mecklenburg felt strong and was in no mood to stop. He had found his rhythm. It was just like leading a cavalry attack. The hooves were pounding and the enemy was in full retreat. Now was the time to complete his assertion of authority and plant the flag on the battlefield.

"One must have experienced the great war to comprehend what is transpiring around us, *meine Herren.*" The count nodded sagely and stroked his mustache.

"*Jawohl, meine Herren,* I have seen too much—*viel zu viel.*"

And then he began reminiscing—about the war, of course—describing the battles of the Marne and the Somme, the ear-shattering bombardments he had experienced on at least nine occasions, his transfer to the eastern front after Brest-Litovsk, his first impressions of Kiew's leafy boulevards in the spring, the strategic challenges of conducting a military campaign in a steppe that constantly resounded with the hooves of anarchist horses, and the truculence of the peasantry, the perfidy of the Austrians, and the unreliability of the Ukrainian nationalists.

As he pretended to listen—there was no harm in feeding the old man's delusions of grandeur—Pieracki rubbed his stomach and felt it tighten painfully.

"Will they never feed us?" he said as soon as the German had finished.

"Why would they? Food will make us strong and they want

us to be weak. They will charge us with absurd crimes and, if we are weak and hungry, we will sign the confessions and they will blame all their failures on us, on imperialism. Even he," von Mecklenburg pointed at Golub, "will sign. We have all joined the enemies of the people. For good, I fear." He paused deliberately for effect.

"And there is no going back."

Golub shook his head wearily. There was no point in taking the Nazi's bait and pursuing the class struggle on the bourgeoisie's terms. It was far better to ignore the Prussian and demonstrate that he, like all good Bolsheviks, was impervious to his desperate jabs. Golub tossed his coat on the bench, threw back his head, inhaled and exhaled loudly, and proceeded to do knee bends. After the tenth, he stopped abruptly and grabbed his wet forehead. He closed his eyes tightly and lowered his head.

"You should conserve your strength, Herr Journalist."

"It is nothing—momentary blackness in the eyes. It will go away."

As he opened his eyes and took a step forward, however, Golub lost his balance, did a half-pirouette like a boxer who'd just taken a sock to the jaw, and slammed his head hard against the concrete wall. He slumped to the ground between the bench and the shit bucket and a trickle of dark blood began flowing behind his left ear and down the side of his neck. He shook his head and applied a crumpled handkerchief to the wound. Relentlessly, a red blot spread across the white cloth.

"Permit me to take a look," Pieracki said. "I have some experience with medicine. My father was a doctor."

"It is nothing." Golub waved him away with a desultory motion of his right hand. "I only need to rest. I am tired. That is all."

Pieracki persisted. "Here: place the sleeve of your coat against the wound. It will stem the blood flow." He glanced at the gash in Golub's head.

"This is serious, *mon ami*. You need stitches."

"Stitches?" von Mecklenburg exclaimed. "Who needs stitches in the grave?"

*

The steady trickle of blood clotted Golub's hair and drained his face of color, endowing him with an alabaster complexion similar to the perpetual cloud cover outside. He lay on the bench with his eyes closed, his coat slung over his chest, his legs fully extended, his glasses perched crookedly on his nose. His thoughts raced chaotically: from the powerful smell of vinegar in his father's shop to his mother's smothering embraces to his first encounter with socialist pamphlets in the bookstore on Houston to his altercations with the rabbi over the authority of the Torah. When the past halted its relentless assault and he became aware of being conscious, he puzzled over why just these remembrances came rushing back. And then, after so many unrelated memories collected, like rain drops in a dirty can, his mind turned in on itself and, comforted by the recurrent image of the besotted bums on the Bowery, Golub fell into a deep sleep.

The hole in the wall had turned the color of soot. The sun had probably set and a gentle breeze blew into the cell. Von Mecklenburg stood near the gate with his face pressed to the rusty bars. There was no one in the corridor. Indeed, no one had appeared since Pieracki had arrived the day before. Were it not for a diffuse yellow light somewhere to his right, the corridor would have resembled the inside of a mausoleum.

"Hallo!" he cried. "Is anyone there? Hallo! Hallo!"

His voice reverberated weakly and the mournful echo accentuated his sense of solitude and abandonment. The German strained to hear if there was any other sound, but there was none, not even the drip of a leaky pipe. An occasional flicker of the light created the momentary impression of flying bats or scurrying mice. Real vermin would have been almost preferable in this No Man's Land illuminated by dying sulfurous flares.

"We appear," von Mecklenburg announced solemnly, "to be the only cell here. A sign of our exceptional importance?" He knew that was unlikely.

"Or of our complete insignificance?" He took one end of his mustache between his right thumb and forefinger and tugged on it.

"Or have they simply forgotten that we exist?" The count stepped back from the gate and looked inquiringly at Golub.

"He resembles a corpse," the Pole said. "*Est-il mort?*"

"*Non, il vit,*" said von Mecklenburg. "*Il va vivre.* He is breathing regularly, probably dreaming of communism. Look closely. See?"

"Yes, of course, *oczywiście*." Pieracki peered at Golub's face to make sure he was asleep before continuing. "I have known men like him in my country." He shook his head with what appeared to be resignation.

"Fanatics. They know all the words. They have all the answers. They recite all the slogans. But they cannot see the world around them—or the dirt under their fingernails."

"We have them, too," von Mecklenburg sighed. "Such types are everywhere. They are foul little boys. They play at politics, when they should be playing in sand boxes with toy soldiers." The count spread his hands and adopted an exaggeratedly religious tone.

"Forgive them, Lord, for they know not what they do."

"Even the Nazis?"

"Even stupider little boys with guns. That is all they are. We—"

"Who, Herr Graf?"

"The nobility, of course—*der Adel*. We will not allow that absurd little man to destroy the Fatherland."

"Perhaps you underestimate him—and overestimate yourselves?"

"Who built Germany? *Der Adel*. Who made it strong and prosperous? *Der Adel*. It will take more than a brown shirt and a small mustache to destroy it."

"You could be wrong. Look at Italy."

Von Mecklenburg bristled.

"That ridiculous man? How can you compare spaghetti-eaters to *das Volk der Dichter und Denker*?"

"Russia also had its share of poets and thinkers and look at it now." The Pole pointed to the sleeping Golub. "They destroy civilization and they laugh, or sleep, while doing it."

The count's response was immediate.

"Russia is savage—a vast, uncultured, barbarian land. De Custine recognized that with the clarity of a biblical prophet a hundred years ago. I saw it myself when I was here during the war. And the Bolsheviks are Russians, after all. How can they not be savages? It is their Tatar blood." Von Mecklenburg took a deep breath.

"We are Europe. Russia is—"

"Golub is a Jew."

"And he claims to be a journalist. But I doubt it."

"What then?"

"An agent of the Komintern, of course."

"Then why is he here?" Pieracki replied with unfeigned skepticism. "He's right, you know. He *is* their comrade. He doesn't belong here. *He* should be interrogating *us*. He should be drinking vodka with Comrade Stalin in the Kremlin."

"Why is anyone here? But in his case the answer is obvious." Von Mecklenburg took a step forward and lowered his voice as he spoke into Pieracki's ear.

"I would wager my estate that he is an informer."

"That *would* explain the warm coat. Still..."

"And," the count tapped his temple with his forefinger, "his crazy ideas. No Bolshevik is quite that arrogant and obtuse anymore." He adopted a hushed tone again.

"We would do well to humor him. He is obviously hoping to provoke us."

"But if he's a provocateur," Pieracki remarked hopefully, "that must mean the authorities have no evidence against us."

The young Pole's naiveté was astonishing. How could he be a member of the diplomatic corps? How could Warsaw send a boy to do a man's job in a barbaric land that punished ignorance?

"Evidence? What evidence?" Von Mecklenburg's eyes opened wide. "They need no evidence. They can manufacture whatever they want and whatever they need. That is the genius of this system, *mein junger Freund.* They can make you into a Japanese spy, me into a Romanian imperialist, and our sleeping comrade into an agent of Wall Street. And we will believe it, too!"

*

Golub stirred and both men turned in his direction. He had raised his hand to his wound and was moaning.

"Water."

"There is none," Pieracki stated.

"Call"—Golub's voice faltered—"the guards."

"*Wozu?*" Von Mecklenburg exchanged a knowing glance with Pieracki. "Why bother? You know they will not come."

"*Vody!*" This time Golub managed a shout in Russian. "*Vody!*"

"The wall," von Mecklenburg suggested. "Try licking the wall, Herr Journalist. It is moist, especially"—he ran his hand along the concrete beneath the aperture—"*here*."

Golub staggered to his feet. His greatcoat dropped to the floor. He left it lying on the ground and took two uncertain steps toward the wall. His face was white and his hair was thick with blood.

"Here," the count gestured. "It is not *Mineralwasser*, but it will do."

"*Danke*, Nazi."

"*Bitte, tovarishch.*"

Von Mecklenburg held back a smirk. The American Jew was beginning to amuse him. He was an annoying *Menschlein*, of course, but ultimately a harmless clown, like that Mussolini. It was laughable that, even when in such obviously great distress, the little New Yorker should feel impelled to maintain his revolutionary bearing and engage in needless posturing. Surely Golub knew that he was not and could not be a Nazi, if only because a real National Socialist would have long since pummeled him to death. Alas, only a tired nobleman would respond to blatant provocations with wisdom, irony, self-deprecation, and trenchant wit.

The wind began blowing fiercely. Shivering, Pieracki rushed to the bench and, after unbinding his cummerbund, folding it neatly in two, and placing it on the wood, occupied the corner. He drew his knees toward his chin and embraced them with his arms. Golub grabbed his greatcoat and, sidling next to the Pole, motioned von Mecklenburg to sit to his left. Then he said, "You take this end and you take this one," and they placed the huge coat over their heads.

Had he possessed the German's talkative nature, he could've told them about the socialist youth camps in the Catskills, the firing range where the milky-faced boys practiced shooting at targets of fat-cheeked, cigar-smoking monopoly capitalists, and the incessant arguments with his father, the religious pickle dealer who was powerless to prevent his son from turning his back on the ghetto and the synagogue and the business. But it was pointless: they couldn't possibly understand. They were bourgeois capitalists and anti-Semites, while he was a communist and a Jew. They were separated by a Grand Canyon of class, race, and ideology. And besides, the pain in his lung had returned and he could feel the slow movement of thick blood slithering in snake-like fashion down his neck.

At night, as the men slept under their makeshift tent, the siren blared twice. Once, sometime after midnight, a heavy footfall resounded outside, shouting and what may have been whimpering followed, and two bursts of gunfire exploded like thunder. And then the boots crunched through the snow, doors creaked open and were banged shut, and a dog barked—but in the distance, in all likelihood coincidentally. The aperture had disappeared within the coal-like blackness of the cell. Only the wind continued to howl, like a pack of hungry wolves, occasionally injecting flurries of plump snow into the tiny room. By the early morning, when the aperture resembled an empty moving-picture screen, the coat was covered with a thin layer of white fluff. The cell was quiet—almost as quiet as a front-line graveyard, von Mecklenburg might have said—except for the insistent clattering of cold teeth.

*

Von Mecklenburg's eyes opened. He raised his hands carefully and lowered the coat from his head, inhaling the icy air with a greediness that astonished him. The count ran his lifeless tongue along his cracked lips. His mustache extended too far over his upper lip and the stubble on his cheeks had begun to itch. He slipped off his shoes and realized that he had almost no feeling in his frigid toes. He cracked them gingerly; then he rubbed the soles of his feet against each other. They came to life, but remained as cold as before.

The greatcoat expanded and contracted, with Pieracki's regularly paced inhalations and exhalations and Golub's hissing and wheezing. How appropriate that the American, who spoke like a broken record, should breathe like a broken radiator. Von Mecklenburg rose from the bench, lowered his pants, and squatted over the bucket. There was no paper, not even an old newspaper. It was just as in the trenches, but without the bombs, the grenades, the machine guns, the barbed wire, and the mud. The incessant din, the earsplitting roar, the horrific screams had actually been tolerable, at least after a while: one responded to them with a combination of fatalism, indifference, and hope. It was the ubiquitous mud—the slimy, ugly brown concoction of earth, clay, excrement, urine, and water—that had disgusted and repelled him.

Fatalism was powerless to deal with filth. One could always close one's eyes and ears, but how could one close one's touch? After von Mecklenburg was done, he glided his fingers along the snow-covered coat and wiped his hands clean on his trousers.

"Wake up," he said quietly to the others. "We have water."

"*Co?*" The Pole jerked awake. "*Woda?*"

"*Jawohl, Wasser*," replied von Mecklenburg. "The snow— on the coat. Be careful. We can drink it."

Pieracki nudged Golub. The American grunted and smacked his lips. As his head emerged from beneath the coat, he blinked and looked sleepily at von Mecklenburg.

"*Gospodin zhurnalist*," the count said in Russian, "*vot Vasha voda.*"

"*Gde?*" Golub cried. He was fully awake and his wide-open eyes stared at von Mecklenburg in disbelief.

"Where? *Gde?*"

"There—in front of you. See the snow? There's your *voda.*"

The three dropped to their knees and, with each man holding a corner of the coat to produce a taut surface, proceeded to lap up the snow with their leathery tongues and suck greedily on the thick wool. When they were finished, they buried their faces in the fabric that smelled of sweat and smoke and rubbed off the dirt and grime and blood.

The siren's insistent cry dissolved in the wind. The rude thumping of footsteps and the protracted creaking of a heavy gate followed. The sound of congested motors struggling with their loads, of wheels churning up gravel or snow or ice, of dogs yelping and snarling, and of the wind whistling filled the air. Then, to their surprise, the footsteps came nearer, or appeared to come nearer.

"Food." Pieracki's eyes were focused on the aperture.

"More likely a death sentence," von Mecklenburg muttered bleakly.

He went to the gate, placed his left ear against one of the metal rods, frowned meaningfully, and raised a forefinger to his lips. The footsteps appeared to be on their floor, possibly just beyond the corridor to their right.

"Do you hear?" Pieracki whispered. "They're here."

A door groaned and the footsteps receded. The siren continued inciting the dogs, but the corridor leading to the cell remained perfectly silent. To his surprise, and shame, Pieracki could hear his heart beat against his breast. Was that a sign of cowardice? Or were his nerves on edge? He recalled his fear of being called upon by the gnome-like Kowalski and not knowing the third-person plural of *esse*. The memory of Latin class brought a smile to his lips. No, all was well—still. *"Jeszcze Polska nie zginęła"*— the first words of the Polish anthem—coursed through his mind: "Poland still lives on." Indeed, and so did he—still.

Von Mecklenburg interrupted his reverie.

"I suppose we could"—he appeared to be struck by a sudden realization of the obvious—"I suppose we could die here."

The count stared at the darkness and listened, but could hear nothing—no voices, no footsteps, no scurrying of rats, no screams. It was like *Niemandsland* on a moonless night in the middle of winter. Or like the tremulous Ukrainian steppe, just before battle, as the troops attached their bayonets and waited fearfully for the order to attack. Or, he had to smile, just like his estate, when his wife left for the Pomeranian coast with the children and the huge house stood empty, hollow, and quiet for eight delicious weeks and he could savor the silence, take long walks in the cool forest, visit the tavern in town, and get drunk on slivovitz with the Polish laborers and their fat wives.

*

Like a drum roll, Golub's wound throbbed without pause and every movement of his head, however slight, resulted in excruciating pain. The burning sensation in his right lung had also become more acute. He lay on the bench with his spine pressed against the wall, trying to remain as still as possible and breathing in short gulps, as if he had just run up a steep hill in the Catskills, with his gear in his knapsack and a red flag in his right hand, ready to be planted at the apex to mark the revolutionary brigade's victory over imperialism. He would sleep for minutes at a time and then awaken with a jolt, snapping his head back, sometimes knocking it against the concrete and grimacing. He pleaded for water, but there was none, so Pieracki and von Mecklenburg said nothing. Both were quiet—at times, one of them would hum a fragment of some melody and then, after a couple of bars, stop—and only the wind and an occasional dog broke the silence.

Von Mecklenburg took two long strides toward the wall

on his right, stood with his heels pressed against it, and began placing one foot directly in front of the other, heel to toe, heel to toe, heel to toe, until he reached the wall beneath the window. He then stood with his heels against the gate, repeating the maneuver, while pausing momentarily to push the shit bucket to the side. The space was ten foot-lengths long and six wide, almost the exact size of a bunker during the war. When he stood in the middle of the cell and extended his arms, he could almost touch the wall and the gate. Many trenches were about the same width, especially on the eastern front, in Poland and Ukraine, where maneuver trumped position and there was neither time nor need to build the elaborate mazes that crisscrossed Belgium and northeastern France. At least the cell was dry. And the shit bucket, however repulsive, was incomparably more refined than the offal one encountered on the front.

"Have you seen any more?" Pieracki asked reluctantly.

"*Mehr?* More of what?"

"*Ratten.*"

"*Nein, mein lieber Freund,* that was our breakfast, dinner, and supper. Now we must fast—like good Christians."

The Pole held up his hands against the light and shook his head in dismay. He turned them over slowly, as if he were a mime, fascinated by the curious sensation that they were not quite his. The Zbigniew Pieracki he knew had fleshy hands and fingers. These belonged to some emaciated man with torn pants who was rotating his hungry hands before a cold hole in a strange wet wall.

"In a few more days we will resemble the peasants"—von Mecklenburg motioned with his head in the direction of the sky— "out there."

Pieracki lowered his hands, inserted them into his pockets, and shook his head.

"I still remember when I saw my first corpse, lying half on the sidewalk, half in the gutter. No one paid attention to the body. They walked around it, over it, as if it wasn't there. I stopped—I felt I had to stop—and people scowled and told me to get out of their way, to keep moving, that they'd be late for work. I couldn't understand their coldness, their indifference, their inhumanity. Didn't they see? Didn't they care? Why didn't they do something?" He shook his head again.

"*Matko Boska,* how naïve I was! And now, when I see

corpses, I too keep walking." His voice turned to a whisper.

"How quickly one gets used to the misery!"

"*Jawohl.*"

"And to the horror."

"Especially in war," the count said. "We had it better than the enlisted men. They lived like rats. We—"

"—ate rats?"

"*Quelle différence, n'est-ce pas?*"

"At least you ate."

"But the bombs, when they fell, did not differentiate between officers and soldiers."

"And yet," Pieracki said, "you are here, while millions rot in graves."

"*Ç'est vrais,*" von Mecklenburg nodded sadly. "But my country is in ruins. *Tod. Kaputt. Basta.* My Germany is dead. It was crucified, it died, and it was buried—by us, by us Germans. We lost hope and we lost faith." He closed his eyes for several seconds. And then:

"How can a Fatherland exist without its children? We betrayed our own country—*unser eigenes Land.* Not the soldiers, of course. We fought bravely to the very end. But the politicians and, alas, the people. The former are venal—they would sell their mothers' gravestones for a profit—while the latter are cowards." He sighed deeply.

"It was not always like this. But now, today, there is no Germany anymore. It is dead." The count appeared to be thinking.

"*Wer weiss?* Perhaps that little man will help resurrect it."

"Your Herr Hitler craves Poland," Pieracki stated peremptorily. He rose to his feet and stood with his face raised toward the opening.

"We shall fight, you know. Poland always fights."

"*Ich weiss, ich weiss,*" von Mecklenburg said wearily. "But we will not. Germany has no strength left. Who is to march and fire the guns? *Die Mütter? Die Kinder?* The one-legged veterans? The aging nobility and degenerate aristocracy? The corpses?"

"Our mothers and children will fight." Pieracki took a deep breath. "We never surrender, even when we should."

"Then you will fight alone." Von Mecklenburg resumed his pacing. "There will be no more wars, Herr Pieracki, I assure you. War is madness. It is impossible—*vollkommen unmöglich.*" He stood, arms akimbo, in the middle of the cell.

"Look around you, Herr Pieracki, everyone is dying. There is no one left to shoot, or even to be shot. Certainly not in this godforsaken land."

The Pole stared at von Mecklenburg.

"You destroyed it during the war, Herr Graf. My father was here with Piłsudski after the Kaiser's army withdrew. The devastation was total, he said. It was bedlam. The entire country was burning and you Germans lit the fire."

"Did we?" von Mecklenburg asked absentmindedly. "*Jawohl*, I suppose we did. The peasants hated us." He sniffed.

"I cannot blame them, of course. I would not have surrendered my farm either. But it was war and, alas, *Krieg ist Krieg*."

*

The two men stood side by side beneath the window. A cold breeze was blowing, sending gusts of frigid air into the cell. Pieracki rubbed his hands and held them to his face, relishing the brief sensation of warmth. The old German was decent: he could even imagine sharing one—but only one!—glass of wine with him. Unfortunately, this didn't change the fact that he was a relic of the past. His time was gone, over, and it was he who was *tod und kaputt*. His tiresome irony, like his unrealistic views of a world he no longer understood, was characteristic of his effete dying class. Prussian landowners knew how to grow rye, but they were no match for the likes of Hitler and Stalin. Gentility and aristocracy could not defeat brutality. The world would belong to the Golubs as long as the von Mecklenburgs continued to mismanage it and the Pierackis failed to take matters into their own hands.

"Every morning," the Pole carefully pronounced each word, "there are dozens of corpses in front of our consulate."

"What do you do with them?"

"What can we do? At first, we called the authorities, but they never came. Too busy, they said, too many dead. Now we just watch them pile up, until a cart appears and loads them up and disappears. Sometimes, they lie there for days—like refuse."

"At night, the scavengers come and probe their mouths for gold teeth. I have seen them with my own eyes. Sometimes they find a tooth. Sometimes, they strip them of their clothes."

"*Je sais*. And we get used to the naked corpses, too, don't

33

we?"

Von Mecklenburg nodded.

"Man gets used to everything. *Homo homini lupus.*"

How vivid and familiar was the terrible image invoked by the Pole and how often had he seen it on a battlefield after a failed attempt to cross No Man's Land and breach enemy lines. There was nothing left to say in the presence of so much death. Only fatalism, indifference, and a *soupçon* of residual hope enabled one to make sense of such a world. The count shook his head ever so slightly. He knew he could not afford to think that way *here*, in the cell. Hope was imperative. Despair was suicidal. Alas, despair made eminently greater sense than hope, at least today.

The two men took deep breaths of the cold night air and returned to the bench.

"Sit up, Herr Journalist—*bitte!* We want to sleep, too."

*

It was the emphatic banging of the wooden sticks that intruded on their sleep and forced them to pry their heavy eyes open. Five guards, all reeking of a powerful home-brewed *samogon*, had burst into the tiny cell. They were shouting incomprehensibly and smacking the men across their shoulders, arms, and heads. Pieracki and von Mecklenburg jumped to their feet, shielding themselves with their hands, while Golub extended both palms and implored, "Comrades! Stop! Stop! I am one of you! Please, comrades, stop!"

His pathetic entreaties only infuriated the guards and three of them began beating him with renewed vigor. When he dropped to the floor, a guard kicked him in the stomach and he released a sustained groan that hinted at more than just physical anguish. Golub struggled to get to his feet, warding off the blows that rained down on his head, while two guards tied von Mecklenburg's and Pieracki's hands behind their backs with chunks of thick rope. The others shoved the American against the wall and pressed their sticks against his throat. The shit bucket turned over. He gagged and coughed and a stream of blood ran from the corner of his mouth and collected in the stubble on his chin. Then they turned him face to the wall and bound his hands. He tried to speak, to plead his case, to make them understand, but a swift poke in his kidney silenced him in mid-word.

The guards led the men along the dank corridor, through

an open iron door, and down three flights of unwashed stairs that smelled of human excrement, onions, and formaldehyde. Another guard pushed open the heavy wooden door at the foot of the stairs and the prisoners were shoved into the bracingly cold air. Pieracki slipped on the ice and fell and two guards proceeded to beat him savagely with their truncheons.

"*Vstavay, svoloch, vstavay!*" they shrieked until he dragged himself to his feet. "Get up, you bastard, get up!"

The bleak sky was the color of lead: it would be daybreak soon. A black van stood in the courtyard with the words, "Agricultural Products," stenciled on its sides in Russian in unevenly spaced large white letters. One guard jerked open the door and the others pushed the three men inside. The door slammed shut and they found themselves in a foul-smelling, inky space bounded by two tiny shimmering holes on both sides of the van. As their eyes adjusted, they could just make out the uncertain shadow of a man sitting on the floor in a corner on the left.

"*Dobryy den.*" He spoke in Ukrainian. "Good day. Welcome to Ukraine."

*

The guards struck the sides of the van with their sticks, producing rounds of ear-splitting explosions that, like machine-gun fire, shook the vehicle and reverberated chaotically inside. Incapable of moving, Golub released a pitiful groan with every bang. The others bent their bodies inward and remained bowed over until the assault ended, resembling soldiers cowering in a trench during the relentless firing of big guns. Slowly, hesitantly, they leaned back and tried to steady their nerves by taking long, deep breaths. The air was stagnant and it smelled of gasoline and sweat. Golub gasped like a drowning man. Only the Ukrainian remained silent in his corner.

As a siren began to wail, a dog howled, someone shouted, and heavy footsteps crunched through the snow. The two men in the cab exchanged some barely audible words and laughed loudly. The motor roared to life and the van leaped forward. Its wheels turned, whining and wheezing, crushing the ice and snow, and navigating the potholes in the crumbling asphalt. The van swayed from side to side. The men's heads bumped against the walls and Golub resumed his moaning. Furious canine barking merged with a series of gruffly delivered commands and the van came to a halt, its engine idling. The men in the cab said something again, someone snarled what sounded like an order, the main gate creaked open, and the van resumed moving with a sudden jolt. The men fell over on their sides. As the truck made a sharp right onto a larger road and picked up speed, they struggled to sit up.

The ride became smoother, but every encounter with a pothole, rut, or bump dashed the men's heads against the floor. Golub lay whimpering like a wounded animal, while the others twisted and turned, using their bound hands as ungainly levers to lift their torsos from the floor. Von Mecklenburg and the Ukrainian were the first to sit upright; Pieracki, cursing heavily under his breath, was next. The blood from Golub's wound made its way into his eyes and mouth and he coughed repeatedly before finally falling silent.

"He won't make it," Pieracki whispered. He had placed his hand into a pool of Golub's blood and was wiping it against the side of the van.

"And what exactly do you propose we do, *mein lieber Herr*?"

"Nothing—I know."

"Indeed, he may be the lucky one."

Pieracki held his breath as his body trembled.

"*Tak*," he said thoughtfully. "I've heard about the Soviet secret police. Their methods are supposed to be very—"

"—refined." Von Mecklenburg completed the sentence and poked Golub with his leg. There was just enough light to see the rough outline of the supine American.

"Herr Journalist, can you hear us?"

Golub groaned.

"We will push you up with our legs, Herr Journalist. *Sie verstehen?* But you must help—with your hands. Push yourself up with your hands. Understand?"

Golub groaned again.

"*En ensemble*," von Mecklenburg ordered Pieracki. "Place your feet against his right shoulder. Yes, *there*. I'll place mine against his left. Now, on three and we push. One, two, *three!*"

Golub cried out in pain.

"*Tikha, svoloch*," a shout came from the cab. "Quiet, you bastards!"

"*Danke*," Golub said softly.

"You are welcome," von Mecklenburg replied in English.

*

The American was in his place, sitting silently, and the Pole had—
Gott sei dank—finally overcome his nation's ingrained truculence
and was being cooperative. There remained the new man in the
corner and the count addressed him in a curiously accented version
of the central Ukrainian vernacular.

"I fear that we have not been properly introduced. I am
August Graf von Mecklenburg, representative of Germany in the
Ukrainian Socialist Soviet Republic. *A Vy khto*, may I ask? And
who are you?"

"Igor Kortschenko, *Dichter aus Wien*." The man had a
mellifluous voice and he expressed the words as if he were reciting
a poem.

The final scene of *La Bohème* flashed before von
Mecklenburg's eyes and he barely repressed a sardonic rejoinder.
But before he could continue with his questions, a broad smile
enveloped Pieracki's face and, flushed with excitement, he cried
out:

"*Ein Dichter! Wie entzückend!* How delightful! A Viennese
poet!"

And then, fully aware that he was about to act against his
better judgment and follow in the ridiculous old man's footsteps,
the Pole commenced singing, at first quietly and then loudly:

> *Wien, Wien, nur du allein,*
> *Sollst stets die Stadt meiner Träume sein!*
> *Dort, wo die alten Häuser stehn,*
> *Dort, wo die lieblichen Mädchen gehn!*

Pieracki glowed.

"*Was für eine wunderbare Stadt!* What a beautiful city—
Vienna!" He spoke without a trace of irony.

"The waltzes, the cakes, the cafés, the Heuriger, *die Frauen.*
Ja, ja," his voice trailed off, "*das waren die Zeiten…*"

"*Doch*," said Kortschenko, "those were indeed the days,
Herr—?"

"My apologies! My deepest apologies! Once again I have
committed an unpardonable *faux pas*! Pieracki—Zbigniew Pieracki,
Polish diplomat—at your service! It is my honor to make your

acquaintance. You have already been introduced to our good count and the unhappy gentleman in the corner is Mister Golub, a communist, a journalist, and a Jew from New York."

Kortschenko coughed politely.

"You should know, Pan Pieracki"—he purposely used the Polish word for mister—"that I am—"

"—a Ukrainian nationalist?" Pieracki exclaimed. "Have I guessed correctly? Yes, I see from your silence that I have. And do you know how I knew, *mon ami*? You are all so serious. That is how. Forgive me for saying so, but you nationalists are like the communists, *tak, tak*—just like the communists.

"Am I not right, Mister Golub? It is always the nation or the proletariat with you. But tell me, *mes amis*, how can one be a revolutionary in the presence of beautiful women? I cannot speak for New York, but Vienna's—oh, *Matko Boska*, Vienna's may be even more extraordinary creatures than Poland's!"

How could he hold back? How could he say no to Wien's many charms? How could he not proclaim them at the top of his voice, even in the presence of a Wiener who was also an enemy of Poland? Fanaticism was quite out of place here, as were provincial pigheadedness and patriotic obduracy, and Pieracki returned to Rudolf Sieczynski's irrepressible paean to the Habsburg capital:

Wien, Wien, nur du allein
Sollst stets die Stadt meiner Träume sein!

Startled by the Pole's casual dismissal of his politics, Kortschenko listened briefly and then joined in. Why not? His beloved city deserved to be celebrated, even in a prison van hurtling down a country road in Ukraine. And then, to everyone's surprise, von Mecklenburg also began singing. The count's métier was speech, but, notwithstanding his strong preference for the unsung word, it was, he knew, his duty as an officer to add his baritone to the two tenors. Three years at the front had taught him that morale invariably improved when the trench soldiers broke out in song and their officers joyfully accompanied them.

Dort, wo ich glücklich und selig bin,
Ist Wien, ist Wien, mein Wien!

Only Golub remained quiet, dismayed and angered by the sudden onset of merriment and the full-scale reversal of moods. It was as if these gentlemen were sitting around a campfire after a long day's hike, eating hot dogs and marshmallows, and planning a panty raid on the girls' camp down the road. He sniffed. Only the bourgeoisie could make light of the class struggle, even as its vitality was fading and a new class order was emerging throughout the world. It was consoling to know that every note they sang hastened the birth pangs of history.

*

The voice in the cab had resumed shouting, but Golub knew better than to say anything. Let the merrymakers get their comeuppance; let the decadent bourgeoisie feel the people's wrath. Then a fist banged the wooden partition and the van swerved sharply to the right and came to a jarring halt. Von Mecklenburg and Pieracki went flying against the two men in the front. A drawn-out squeaking ensued, snow crunched under heavy boots, and the door to the back of the van was yanked violently open. A pale light came flooding inside and blinded the four men.

"*Kto govoril?*" the guard demanded in Russian. He was tapping his thigh with a menacing club.

"We were all speaking," von Mecklenburg replied with all the insouciance he could muster. He had managed to raise himself to a seated position and looked directly at the guard. Judging by the sour smell of his breath, he suspected that this one, like his comrades in the prison, had also been drinking heavily.

Golub cleared his throat and spoke emphatically and without hesitation.

"*Ya molchal, tovarishch.* I was quiet, comrade. You must let me go, comrade. I am a communist, comrade, and these men"—he motioned weakly at the others with his head—"are Nazis, Piłsudskiite fascists, and Ukrainian bourgeois nationalists. I am—"

"*A ty kto?*" said the guard rudely. "And who are you?"

"*Ya—kommunist. Ya—vash tovarishch!* I am your comrade!"

The guard clambered into the van and spat into Golub's face.

"*Zhid!*"

Then he raised his arm and brought down the truncheon across his head. Golub fell over like a stack of wheat. The guard glared at the others.

"Who else is my comrade? *Kto?* Who else wants to be my

comrade? Huh?"

Kortschenko and Pieracki lowered their eyes, while von Mecklenburg stared at the stout, thick-necked man in an ill-fitting olive-drab uniform and high boots. Why, he thought, did all prison brutes look alike? Soldiers came in all shapes and sizes, but guards seemed to come off some assembly line, regardless of race, religion, or nationality.

"*Deutschland Schwein!*"

The guard caught his look, spat, and took another swing, delivering a glancing blow across von Mecklenburg's teeth. The count cried out, while Kortschenko and Pieracki closed their eyes and winced. The guard poked Kortschenko in the belly and, as the Ukrainian gagged, he turned and hit Pieracki sharply across the chest. The Pole released a deep gasp and pulled his head back, striking the side of the van with a thud.

The guard stepped back and tapped his truncheon against the palm of his left hand. He slammed the door shut, lumbered to the cab, and banged the partition with his fist, this time with somewhat less force. His point had been made. The vermin would be quiet, if they knew what was good for them. The motor ignited with a sickly cough and the truck turned into the road. As it accelerated, the van passed a column of armed men leading two long rows of collective farmers clad in colorless coats, with their feet wrapped in rags. The unshaven peasants, their listless eyes set deeply in their sockets, their lips wafer-thin and cracked, silently watched the truck rumble past and spray them with mud and pebbles. The sky had the sallow complexion of a hopeless alcoholic and far above the horizon there flew a flock of birds: tiny specks moving to the left, upward, and back to the right in the manner of a swarm of mosquitoes on a hot summer day.

*

The four men were silent. Golub's head was bleeding profusely from both sides now and, with his hands tied behind his back, there was nothing he could to do to stem the flow. Von Mecklenburg's upper lip was torn. He had lost three front teeth, which he spat out and heard fall to the metal floor. Kortschenko and Pieracki eyed each other's ghostly outlines.

"Pssst, Pan Kortschenko, try to untie me." It was the Pole. "They bound us quickly and they were drunk. It may be a simple knot and with a little luck..."

The Ukrainian nodded and the two men began turning in their places. Once their backs faced each other and their fingers grazed the floor, they pushed themselves with their feet until their hands touched. Pieracki's hunch had been correct and, after fumbling with the thick rope, Kortschenko's stiff fingers finally succeeded in loosening the knot. The Pole shook off the rope and, careful not to strike the sides or roof of the van, extended his arms above and in front of his head. They felt as light as wings and he almost succumbed to the urge to flap them madly.

"*Mir auch, bitte.*"

"You tend to the Jew," Pieracki said after untying Kortschenko, "and I'll look after the German."

Von Mecklenburg applied a silk handkerchief to his bleeding lips and thanked the gods for the Slavic love of alcohol. After passing his hand along the floor, he collected the missing teeth and dropped them into his pants pocket.

"Air," he choked, "I need air—*Luft.*"

How fortunate that Soviet trucks were so poorly constructed, with holes or cracks where screws had fallen out or the welding had been done sloppily. If this were Germany, they would be sitting in total darkness, with their hands bound tightly, and their disorientation would be complete. He placed his lips over the tiny hole near his shoulder and inhaled. The air outside was cold and he drank it in as if it were a tall beer on a summer afternoon in Wannsee. When he was sated, von Mecklenburg pressed an eye to the hole.

"Where are we? Can you see where we are?" Kortschenko whispered. "We've left the city, haven't we?" He was squeezing his fingers and making fists. The blood had returned to his hands and they prickled and itched unbearably.

"It is all white," von Mecklenburg murmured, "all white. There is nothing but snow."

"Of course, we are in the countryside. Are we going east or south?"

"East, I think."

"Are they taking us to Russia?" Pieracki asked.

"But we might also be going south," von Mecklenburg added. It was painful to talk and he held his tongue against his upper lip.

"It is impossible to tell. I cannot see the sun. The sky is all white—all white clouds." He paused again, this time to suck on his upper lip.

"Everything is white—*alles*. I cannot see anything. *Alles ist weiss—ganz weiss.*"

Pieracki pressed his eye to the hole on the other side.

"*Rien,*" he concurred. "There is nothing. It is white—all white, everywhere." He then scuttled toward Golub, still lying in a daze in the corner nearest the cab.

"Come, *mon ami*, turn your back toward me."

"Leave me alone," Golub groaned, with equal measures of misery and defiance.

"But why?"

"I am innocent."

Pieracki placed a hand on Golub's shoulder. "Come, *mon ami*, be sensible. Turn your back. Let me untie you. You will be more comfortable."

Golub wanted to shriek, to scream, to howl—but all he could manage was a feeble whimper: "In the company of fascists, I prefer to remain a prisoner."

"*Comme vous voulez*—as you wish." The American's maddening combination of impotence and blustering was beyond his understanding and, for a moment, Pieracki didn't know what to say next. And then:

"My apologies, *mon ami*, but you are either a bigger fool than I thought or a fiendishly clever provocateur."

"*Me? A provocateur?*" Golub tried to push Pieracki away with his leg. "The Ukrainian—that one, *there*, the anti-Semite. *That* is your provocateur! And the Prussian—"

"Quiet!" von Mecklenburg hissed through his broken teeth. "If your communist friend comes again, he will beat you to death."

"Let him!" Golub managed to raise his voice. "Let him come and see how fascists squirm when faced with Soviet justice! I fear no—"

Before Golub could finish, Kortschenko and Pieracki threw themselves on him. The Ukrainian wrapped his arm around his chest, while the Pole slapped his right hand over his mouth. To their surprise, Golub, instead of resisting, began singing "The Internationale."

Arise ye workers from your slumbers

Arise ye prisoners of want

Das war zu viel. The communist's impudence had exceeded
all decency and was a deliberate outrage against the memory of the
millions of heroes who had fought for the Fatherland and fallen in
the war. The German formed his hands into a tight ball and
brought them down swiftly and hard against Golub's stomach. His
singing stopped at once and the count stuffed his bloody
handkerchief into the American's mouth.

"You can let him go," he said. "He will not disturb us
anymore."

*

Golub lay quietly, struggling to breathe through his congested nose.
Kortschenko and Pieracki crawled back into their corners.
Distraught at his lack of self-control—striking a prisoner was
coward's play, even if the Bolshevik provoked and fully deserved
it—von Mecklenburg placed his eye to the peephole again. Hoping
to dispel the suffocating sense of dishonor that threatened to
overwhelm his conscience, he kept his eye shut. What better way to
see that his world was vanishing? He felt it with every passing day.
The time of the barbarians had arrived and salvation would come
from the vulgar and the venal.

What place was there for a nobleman in a world such as
this? His estate had been plundered; his family had been killed and
he did not even know when or by whom. He would keep on
serving the Fatherland, as had his fathers and forefathers. That was
his duty. That was his responsibility. After all, the *Vaterland* needed
him. He opened his eye reluctantly and, despite his best efforts not
to see it, the relentless whiteness of the white snow and sky stared
back at him with a ruthlessness, savagery, and indifference that
took his breath away. Or did he, perhaps, need the *Vaterland* more
than it needed him? What should an old soldier do then? Hope for
a new war? Fight another battle? Sacrifice his life for the *Volk*, if
not for its so-called Führer? And who would fight with him? The
mothers, the children, the corpses, and the maimed? When life
resembled—indeed, when it had become—a canvas by Grosz,
what room was there for honor?

"White—it is all white," he muttered. "Even the sky. *Alles
ist weiss.*"

"Can you see any houses, Herr Graf?" Kortschenko asked.

43

It took von Mecklenburg several seconds to realize that the question had been directed at him.

"Yes, but they appear to be empty. No smoke, no people, no life, *nichts*. Absolutely nothing. Just this accursed white."

"Animals?"

"No, nothing. There is nothing but snow—nothing but white snow—*nichts ausser diesem verdammten Schnee*. And white sky."

It seemed self-evident to von Mecklenburg that the appallingly white whiteness of the white snow and white sky was intolerable. It was arguably worse than the carnage—the brown dirt and red blood—of the front. Where was one to go in a world without dimensions, in a world of emptiness? Where could one find refuge or comfort in a hollow world, one without color, without honor, without purpose, without nuance, without substance? What place was there for him in a world such as this? The questions, alas, were rhetorical and he knew that he knew the answers.

*

The van rocked from side to side, swerved to the right like a snake, and bounced to a full stop near the side of the road. Von Mecklenburg, Pieracki, and Kortschenko tumbled to the floor and listened as gears were shifted and the ignition was turned off with a loud click. Then they heard both doors swing open and the driver and guard leap down from the cab into the hard snow.

The two men strode stiffly to the snow banks to relieve themselves. After they buttoned their trousers, they stretched their arms and legs, craned their necks, and cracked their knuckles. The air was cold, but invigorating. The guard leaned against the warm hood, while the driver climbed inside the cab and returned with a bottle of vodka, two dented metal cups, and a small package. He arrayed the objects on the hood, snapped the twine with a quick jerk of his pocket knife, and hurriedly unwrapped the newspaper. A piece of fat, a chunk of gray bread, and a small onion lay before them. He sliced the fat into irregularly shaped pieces and even wiped away a tear as he worked on the onion. Then the two men alternated bites of fat with bites of bread or onion, shots of vodka, and the salacious smacking of greasy lips.

Snow-covered fields extended on both sides of the unpaved road. They rose gently, culminating in a verdant pine forest some one hundred meters on the left and a clutch of white thatched-roof houses about fifty meters on the right. The huts were silent and no hint of smoke escaped from the chimneys. A tiny orchard consisting of hunchbacked apple trees stood to the left of the houses and a row of curiously silent tar-black crows sat on the limb of a solitary oak tree. There was no sign of human life on either side of the road. As the two men ate, an emaciated brown dog with a large red sore on its snout and a drooping tail approached them from the direction of the huts. It sat some five meters away and watched, its head cocked inquisitively to one side.

The men raised themselves from the floor and propped up the inanimate Golub in the corner. His head was draped in blood and this time he neither resisted nor spoke. Kortschenko and Pieracki sat back against the sides of the van, with the ropes tied loosely around their hands, while the count crawled into the corner opposite Golub and nursed his wounded lip. The Pole pressed his eye to the peephole on the right, the Ukrainian to the one on the left. They heard the dog whining and then they heard a gunshot. The crows shrieked and flapped their wings above the orchard trees and then returned to their branch.

The driver crushed the newspaper into a ball and threw it into the snow. He tossed the empty vodka bottle in the direction of the huts. The guard then walked to the snow bank and relieved himself again. As he turned, his left foot tripped over a hard object and, with his right arm extended and his fingers splayed, he slipped and fell into a mound of snow.

"*Blyad!*" he cried. "Shit!"

As he rose to his feet, he extricated his hand from what had felt like a rotting pile of branches, twigs, and leaves and discovered that he was holding a bit of bone in his fist. It was curved and black and could have been a baby's rib.

"*Smotri,*" he grinned at the driver. "Look."

"*Eta tolka kulak,*" the driver grumbled. "It's only a kulak." He motioned at the snow banks with his head—"There are many rich peasants hiding from Soviet power under the snow"—and snickered. "That's where they belong, *svoloch.*" He looked in the direction of the huts.

"Did I ever tell you about the kulaks in my village? We took their grain and their clothes and we drove them bare-assed to the cemetery."

The guard snorted.

"Most of them joined the collective farm voluntarily that day," the driver continued. "See, Izya? We achieved success without violence and"—his smile revealed a row of straight white teeth—"without dizziness."

"Do we have time?" the guard asked, pointing at the settlement with the rib. "These kulaks are rich. I hear they hide gold in the walls of their houses."

The driver looked thoughtfully at his watch.

"Why not? *Pochemu nyet?* We can easily make up the time."

*

An hour later, the two men trudged back to the road through the waist-high snow. Each was carrying two to three icons in his arms. They reached the van sweating and out of breath and dropped the icons on the snow. They stood silently, hunched over, their hands on their trembling knees, and breathed deeply, waiting for their palpitating hearts to return to their normal rhythms. Then the driver disappeared in the cab, while the guard leaned against the side of the van and lit a crumpled cigarette. A minute later the driver reappeared with another bottle in his hand. The guard's eyes glowed. The driver filled both cups to the rim and, as the oily surface of the liquid shimmered in the afternoon light, the two men downed them in one swift motion.

"Do we have any more onions?"

"*Nyet.*"

"Too bad."

"*Da.*"

"Bread?"

"*Nyet.*"

"A pickled tomato would be good."

"*Da.*"

"Fat?"

"*Nyet.*"

"Nothing?"

"*Nichevo.*"

"Come, sit down." The guard placed the icons face-up on the ground. "We should rest our legs before we go." As the driver refilled their cups, the guard added: "The kulaks must have buried the gold in the fields." He spat.

"I tell you, Vanya, these Ukrainians are worse than Jews." The driver nodded.

"But you know what, Izya? I love the peace and quiet here. It used to be you couldn't go down this road without hitting a chicken. Now—look. Nothing. Just us and nature." He had a serene, almost dreamy, expression on his face.

"And you know what, Izya? I love the snow. Most people don't like the snow, but I do. I love it. And you know why, Izya? The snow calms my nerves—that's why. And you know what else, Izya? It hides the filth, all this kulak filth, and it makes the vodka taste better."

"Everything makes vodka taste better, Vanya." The guard chuckled and gestured lamely at the fields. "If you ask me, you can keep your snow. I'll take the gold." He frowned and looked wearily at the van.

"I should take a look at the prisoners. They're too quiet."

"Let the dead bury the dead, Izya. Two more hours and they won't be our problem anymore. Here—have a hundred grams." The driver poured the vodka and re-corked the bottle with a grunt.

"For later."

"I'm surprised they don't smell," the guard said, pointing at the spot where he fell. "They should, shouldn't they? And," he chuckled again, "not just because they're kulaks."

"It's the snow, Izya—and the ice. It keeps them preserved, like mastodons. I told you: that's why I love the snow. In the spring, Izya, that's when it'll smell to high heavens. In the spring, if we come here again, no rest stops for us."

*

Kortschenko kept his eye pressed to the pinhole. There was nothing to see, just as the count had said, nothing but the unforgiving whiteness of the dead snow and the wavering black smear of the pine forest. Mercifully, the woolen sky was a drab white that shaded into gray in places. At times, a bird or two— perhaps a vulture or a hawk—appeared above the forest, circled lazily, and then disappeared beyond the trees. Even more mesmerizing than the milky *Landschaft* was the all-encompassing silence. Except for the strikingly banal conversation between the guard and the driver and the occasional cawing of a bored crow, there was absolutely nothing to be heard, not even the humming of flies or the buzzing of mosquitoes. Everything is dead, he thought, *alles ist hin, tout est mort, vse mertve*. Ukrainians were known for their singing, but no one sang anymore and even the songs had died. Were the animals and insects also dead? And what of the worms? Were they dead or were they feasting on the dead?

How different was this lifelessness from the vibrant villages of Galicia or Niederösterreich which boiled over, even in winter, with myriad sights and sounds and smells. Here was the severe stillness, not of the graveyard, but of the abandoned graveyard. He had occasionally come upon such cemeteries—their crosses tilted, their monuments chipped and broken and lying on their backs like *clochards*, their graves covered with dark moss and waist-high weeds—in his wanderings through the Steiermark and the Waldviertel and they had never failed to fill him with a deeply unsettling foreboding. When even death didn't seem to matter, what chance was there for the living?

It was impossible to tell where they were. The road was unpaved, but most of Ukraine's roads were unpaved. The slate sky was uniformly somber, with few shades or tones, and the sun could be sequestered anywhere. It might be possible, in two or three hours, to tell just where it would set, but even that was doubtful given the impenetrable thickness of the dreadful clouds and the deceptive way in which they diffused the light. They could be anywhere, Kortschenko concluded, or they could just as easily be nowhere. He suspected and feared it was the latter. They were being driven from someplace to someplace, but it really didn't matter, in a bleak wasteland such as this, where they were and where they were going. Wherever they were, wherever they would arrive, it would still be a wasteland.

The irregularly distributed piles that lined the road for kilometers on end were the only objects that stood out against the deadening uniformity of the barren landscape. At first, Kortschenko paid no attention to them, but, after the driver and guard spoke of corpses, it dawned on him that each pile probably contained at least one dead Ukrainian peasant. Directly across from the van was a group of three or four piles, presumably a family; to its left and right were five isolated piles. All of them had obviously been on the way from somewhere to somewhere. And all of them had breathed their last breath in this whitewashed desert. Their villages could not be too far away, which meant that the road passed through countryside populated—or formerly populated—by living human beings now reduced, not even to numbers, but to little disruptions of the smooth surface of the snow.

Kortschenko directed his gaze at the piles in front of him. Whoever they were, they appeared to have huddled together, possibly fallen asleep, and then frozen. There was something black at the foot of one of the piles. Was it a shoe? A bag of some kind? A rock? A log? Or, Kortschenko was repulsed by the thought, a rotting limb or head? The dark object appeared to twitch, almost imperceptibly. Was it still alive? Was the rotting peasant struggling to live? Or was the whiteness of the snow playing tricks on his eye? Kortschenko pressed his other eye to the hole. The glare momentarily blinded him, but once his vision adjusted to the light, he was certain he saw nothing. The piles were immobile. Immersed in the ubiquitous gloom of this awful wasteland, he had obviously imagined the movement of some rotting body part.

After all, this wouldn't be the first time that his imagination had run away with him. He recalled climbing Mount Rax in the summer heat and struggling to reach the snow-covered plateau surrounding Otto-Haus in four or five hours. Vienna had been stifling: the horse manure had appeared to bake in the sun and even the young wine of his favorite Heuriger garden had lost its sweetness and tasted like old vinegar. They sat, exhausted and wet from the torrents of sweat that engulfed their bodies, on the stone terrace overlooking the valley and drinking Enzian and beer; and he swore he saw a mountain goat prancing through the tangled brush on the far side of the barren hill, near the lazy orange glow of the setting sun. But Gabi, Hannes, and Christl had all roared with merriment: "Our poet is seeing things again! Come, Igor, you need another Enzian!" He realized just how hungry he was.

They had arrested him three-four-five days ago, while he was resting comfortably in the express train to Kharkiv and composing a sonnet. They gave no explanation, only barking in a language he did not understand, and kicked him off the train at some abandoned village station with cracked tiles, broken windows, dank weeds, and the intrusive smell of stale urine. They beat him, ceaselessly, for what seemed like days in an adjacent building where the floorboards creaked with every blow and the grimy windows rattled every time he screamed. He was an emissary of the Organization and they knew it, asking him to state, exactly, just who his Ukrainian émigré comrades in Vienna, Prague, Lviv, Kraków, and Berlin were and just what the Organization had entrusted him with accomplishing in the Soviet Motherland. They broke him—after all, he was a *Kaffeehaus-Literat* and not a soldier like the others in his group—and he had signed a long confession in the vain hope that they would let him board the first train home. He recalled fainting, begging for food and water, and then, after spending a day or two on the cold floor of a cold cell expecting to be released, being shoved into this cold van.

"Do you see anything?" someone said. Kortschenko turned his head. It was von Mecklenburg.

"Only snow and corpses, I think."

"They are dying like flies."

"Yes," Kortschenko noted dryly and returned to the hole.

How curious that there should be no flies. Was that because it was winter? He could not remember seeing flies in the wintertime in Vienna, but then again he had never cared to notice or had reason to care to notice. Surely there must have been some amid the horse manure where the Fiaker drivers parked their carriages. But how would he know? The Vienna of the working class and its beasts of burden was not his Vienna. *That* Vienna, *his* Vienna, was the city of songs—the city of music and culture and balls and cafés that so enamored the slippery Pole. What was he doing here—in the middle of nowhere and as far as one could possibly be from his native city? It really made no sense; *es machte überhaupt keinen Sinn*. Poets weren't fighters. He should've known that. Poets were sensitive beings who needed to be coddled and pampered and adored.

The motor roared to life and the truck lurched forward. Once again, the dark object at the foot of one of the piles appeared to twitch. This time, Kortschenko knew it was only an illusion, sparked by the whiteness, the sudden movement of the van, and his own exaggerated fears about the dead Ukrainians in the snow and the still living Ukrainian observing them and hoping—perhaps even praying—that they would not move, never ever move, and that he would find his way home and never ever have to leave it again.

*

The road had lost all semblance of flatness and, as the driver struggled to avoid the ruts and holes and bumps, the van bounced and rocked like a small boat being battered by high storm waves. Golub's head struck the side of the van and, with each knock, he groaned like a wounded soldier on the front. Although von Mecklenburg's thoughts flitted randomly from the war to the van and back to the war again, he was surprised to find himself fixated on Golub's pitiful moans. Alas, there was nothing to be done and nothing to be said in the presence of a body's determined retreat into *Nichtsein*. Golub groaned again. The handkerchief was no longer necessary. Von Mecklenburg withdrew it and the American responded with a hushed "*spasiba*" and an extended moan.

"You need your hands, Herr Journalist"—the German undid the rope—"even if you are a Bolshevik and we are all Nazis."

Golub lay on the vibrating floor, shivering, swallowing the fetid air with his numb mouth, unable to lift his lifeless arms or hands. He tried moving the forefinger and thumb of his right hand, then of his left, and, when he finally felt an unpleasant tingle that heralded a return of sensation, he brought his fingers together in a loose fist. He tried raising his shoulders to his ears, at first without success; then, after repeated attempts, he managed to lift and twirl them, forward and backward. With each movement, he groaned or, if the pain was too great, too piercing, suppressed a groan. Von Mecklenburg watched with his finger to his lips. After a short while, Golub was able to sit up and bring his hands to his swollen face. He carefully extended his fingers to the two gashes, feeling the dry coat of hardened blood on his temples and the stickiness of his clotted hair. The wounds burned and he refrained from touching them. Instead, he began rubbing his temples, cautiously and deliberately. It was only then that the fire in his lung began to interfere with his breathing. He gasped like a fish, producing a raspy sucking sound.

"How do you feel?"

Golub's attempt at a laugh turned into a hacking cough. The count tapped him gently on the back.

"You must be perfectly quiet. You know what will happen if the guard finds us without our hands tied. He will beat us, but you will not survive."

"*Da.*" Golub spoke without emotion. "Perhaps that would

be better." Dimly aware of resembling his father in prayer, he rocked his head from side to side with his eyes closed and his hands on his cheeks.

"After all, what is the point?"

Von Mecklenburg raised his eyebrows. Pieracki leaned toward him and whispered "*incroyable*" into his ear. Equally quietly, the count replied, "*Vraiment.*"

If Golub heard their exchange, he said nothing.

*

The others sat in silence, while Kortschenko gazed through the peephole. The countryside had become less flat, with gently sloping hills, some wooded and some naked, disrupting the monotony. Every few minutes clusters of snow-covered huts appeared, all as apparently devoid of life as those near where the van had stopped. Invariably, the huts were accompanied by visibly neglected orchards, while the fields were barren, except for lonely crows and the remnants of battered scarecrows. Once, he thought he saw a pack of wolves in the distance, near a patch of tall birch trees, but they could also have been stumps or bushes or perhaps even birds. The little piles still lined the road, but irregularly, sometimes appearing in groups, sometimes being absent or invisible for kilometers on end. Evidently, entire families or even villages had set out and dropped dead from cold or exhaustion or both. Why hadn't they fought with their pitchforks and scythes in the time-honored manner of East European peasants? Why hadn't they resisted the Russian communist onslaught? Had every dead Ukrainian peasant killed just one Bolshevik, Stalin would not have survived and Europe could breathe easier, having one less madman to worry about.

The road had become an obstacle course, sometimes forcing the driver to slow down to a crawl. Even then, the van would sink into depressions and ruts and, wheels whirring, motor roaring, and exhaust coughing, slowly, painfully emerge from them. "*Blyad!*" they heard the driver swear. As the van picked up speed, the guard shouted encouragement, "*Davay, davay,* Vanichka!" There were as yet no shadows, but the snow was progressively acquiring a grainy quality, as in an old daguerreotype. The sun was about to set—though just where it was still remained a mystery—and the resulting blackness would make driving doubly difficult.

"The comrades," Kortschenko announced to the others, "appear to be late."

The van rattled along. Vanya the driver had obviously decided to ignore the potholes and hope for the best. "*Kharasho, kharasho*," they heard Izya the guard intone every few seconds. At one point, the van dove into a small pit with a loud bang and the men were thrown at least ten centimeters into the air. Golub groaned.

"It's nothing—*nichevo*. Keep on going, Vanya"—the guard was shouting—"just keep on going. Faster, Vanya, go faster. We'll soon be there. *Davay*, Vanichka, *davay, davay, davay!*"

Kortschenko and Pieracki watched the charcoal-colored countryside rush by. The snow and sky had merged into a blur that, with every minute, became grayer and darker. The driver had turned on the flickering yellow headlights and, when night had fallen and the truck went into curves, they could see the snow banks crazily illuminated, almost as if a ballerina with a lantern were doing a mad dance. At one point, just as they entered a stretch of straight road, Pieracki caught a fleeting glimpse of a sign, but just what it said was impossible to tell.

"*Davay*, Vanichka, *davay!*" were the last words the men heard before the van swerved to the right, went into a violent spin, crashed into something—a fence, perhaps, or a tree—tipped over and proceeded to roll down thunderously what must have been a ravine. It came to rest on its back, its wheels spinning, in the middle of a frozen stream. The lights blinked and then went out. As the wheels came to rest, the silence of the countryside returned and, together with the moonless sky, enveloped the truck and its inhabitants in an impenetrable tomb.

*

Pieracki stirred as a piercingly bright shaft of white light shone directly on his right eye. He turned his head away and saw that he was enmeshed within a pile of limbs, heads, and torsos. The German lay to his right, the Ukrainian to his left, and the hard body beneath his had to be the Jew. Pieracki slid off Golub's abdomen and landed on his knees. Then he examined himself in the glare of the light. His right shoulder and right knee ached, but nothing appeared to be broken. Only the dried blood on his lips and chin indicated that his nose had bled during the night. It was a wonder that he hadn't choked.

There had obviously been an accident. He vaguely recalled a flying sensation followed by an explosion. They had spun over, their bodies had rattled in the van like dried beans in a can, and then he remembered nothing. The door had sprung open during the fall—inadvertent testimony, he thought, to the abysmally poor quality of Soviet-made locks—and Pieracki could see a bright blue, pellucid sky outside. He listened for suspicious noises or familiar voices, but could hear nothing. He crouched, rose to his feet, and, with his head bent, one hand shielding his eyes, and the other stretched out before him like a blind man's cane, gingerly neared the door. Someone groaned. He placed both hands on the door frame and cautiously stepped outside onto a glistening sheet of silvery ice.

They were at the bottom of a small ravine. Above, to his right, was a short wooden bridge. They must have tumbled down the river bank just before crossing it. The driver had probably accelerated at precisely the time that the van had encountered a slick patch of some kind. Or maybe Vanya had had too much to drink and had lost control of the vehicle. It was no use speculating. All that mattered was that there had been an accident and that he was alive.

Pieracki crept along the side of the van like a thief. When he reached the cab, he saw the driver, Vanya, pinned against the door like a butterfly, with a deep red gash running diagonally across his forehead. His face was covered in congealed blood and he did not appear to be breathing. The guard, Izya, had been catapulted through the windshield and his battered and bloody head protruded grotesquely through the broken glass. He was clearly dead. Pieracki climbed inside and, balancing himself carefully on the door frame, placed his finger on the driver's pulse. He was alive, after all, though just barely. There was nothing to be done about him: he would soon be joining Comrade Izya. It occurred to Pieracki that Izya was probably Jewish. What an irony! Did Golub suspect who his tormentor was? He took a careful step backward and climbed out of the cab. It was only then that he realized that the van was lying upside down.

*

The Pole returned to the back of the truck and looked inside. All three men were awake, though groggy. Von Mecklenburg was sitting cross-legged, like an inebriated Indian chieftain, rubbing his neck. Kortschenko was cradling his left hand, which appeared to be broken. Golub had managed to raise himself to his knees, but his forehead, eyes, and cheeks were wet with blood. The American looked exactly like the redskins that adorned the Karl May novels he used to devour as a boy. Was that why the count had struck him as an Indian as well? How odd, Pieracki thought, how truly odd that his current travails were leading him to unearth long-forgotten memories, almost as if his subconscious had embarked on an autobiographical accounting of his lived life.

"They are dead," Pieracki proclaimed without emotion. "Well, the guard is. Comrade Vanya may still have a breath within him. In any case, *mes amis*, it appears that we are free. Upside down, bruised, battered, and lost, but free."

Golub was incredulous.

"Free? And what do you mean by upside down?"

"Yes, quite. We can go wherever we like and do whatever we like. I believe that is the definition of freedom. As to upside down, come outside and see for yourselves."

The three men stepped out of the van and, shading their eyes from the distressingly bright sun, regarded the extraordinary intensity of the sky's blueness with a mixture of surprise and awe, almost as if, it seemed to Pieracki, they were primitive men experiencing their first encounter with civilization. Tears filled their eyes and they lowered their sight to the steeply sloped ravine before turning to face the overturned van. A frail breeze was blowing, stirring up small clouds of powdery snow. Three crows were fidgeting on the bridge, observing the men and occasionally exercising their wings.

The men leaned against the van with their pale, hungry, bearded faces raised toward the sun. They breathed deeply, producing thick billows of condensed air as they exhaled. The cold air invigorated their tired and oxygen-deprived bodies, but it also intensified the pain in their stomachs and reminded them that they both required nourishment and would not get it. Hoping to arrest the nauseating sensation of twirling like a top, Golub pressed his head against the side of the van to steady himself.

"Perhaps we should wait here," he said plaintively, "until someone comes."

"And drags us back to some disgusting cell?"

Kortschenko's mood had noticeably improved now that the white landscape and the foul memory of the sour-tasting wine had disappeared.

"*That*, comrade, is not for me. I prefer sunlight"—his eyes sparkled—"except, of course, when I am drinking a fine Riesling in a wine cellar."

Golub spoke with both eyes closed. "And where are we to go?" He sighed loudly.

"And how far do you think our legs will carry us?"

Kortschenko took a few steps from the truck and peered down the length of the ravine.

"We can follow this stream," he said. "It will take us to some settlement, where they will have food and shelter. Besides, what is the alternative?"

"We could hope for the mercy and wisdom of Soviet power."

Golub walked to the river bank, sat on a large rock, and removed a shoe. The others watched him. Was the American serious, Kortschenko thought, or did he detect a note of irony in his choice of words?

"If we stay, we die," the Pole declared calmly. "If we go, we may not die. It is a question of certainty versus bad odds. If we were at the races, the choice would be obvious."

Golub struggled to his feet.

"Is there water in the stream?" he asked. "My head—I must stop the bleeding. And," he added, almost as an afterthought, "drink."

*

Variously shaped stones, silver, brown, and speckled in color, lay trapped beneath twenty to thirty centimeters of ice; long thin reeds protruded through the sparkling surface, especially along the jagged edges near the shoreline. The four men knelt on both sides of the stream and struck the ice with rocks. They cradled the ice splitters in their hands, as if they were precious stones, and lapped up the moisture with their desiccated tongues and smeared it on their calloused faces. Golub applied the ice to his wounds, while Kortschenko held his broken left hand against the frozen stream and winced.

56

"You," von Mecklenburg turned to Pieracki, "should take the guard's pants. They are no good to him anymore."

"His socks, Herr Graf, could be of use to you and—"

"We should also take their belts," the count continued. "My pants are barely holding up."

"—their coats and weapons," Kortschenko said. "Take them, too."

Von Mecklenburg looked intently at his shrunken abdomen and shook his head in dismay. He had not been this thin since the war. His body was vanishing before his very eyes and he was ceasing to exist as flesh and blood. What would be left of him in a week? Some skin, some bones, a scraggly beard, and desperate and hungry eyes? And then, at some later point that, *Gott sei dank*, was indeterminate, the eyes would be extinguished and nothing would remain, except, perhaps, for his vaporous immortal soul. It would be like experiencing a direct hit by a large shell. Only the smoking crater testified to the existence of the human being who had been obliterated by the explosion.

Golub clasped his aching head with both hands. He had managed to clean most of the blood from his face, which now looked even more pallid and fatigued than before. He eyed the others disapprovingly. They were talking about two dead comrades as if they had just lynched some Negroes and were deliberating how to divide their meager belongings while the bodies still swayed limply in the breeze. He placed no store in bourgeois notions of morality, of course, but such talk was inexcusable, as well as counter-revolutionary. There was a price to be paid for reactionary behavior and these gentlemen would pay it.

Kortschenko, Pieracki, and von Mecklenburg shuffled along the ice toward the cab. A menacingly black oil stain glowed beneath the engine. A crow was sitting on the guard's head and poking at his eyes with its beak. It flew to the bridge above, cawing and flapping its wings loudly, as soon as it saw the three men approach. As they peered inside the cab, the driver opened one eye. It was encrusted in blood, but he succeeded in blinking once.

"He has a pulse," Pieracki said. "Just barely."

"Leave him," Kortschenko declared coldly. "He is our enemy. *Der ist unser Feind.* By the way," he added, "both comrades have guns." He pocketed one and gave the other to von Mecklenburg.

The dead guard's body had begun to harden and his limbs refused to yield easily to their attempts to extricate them from his garments. After ten minutes of tugging, Pieracki finally pulled off his coat. The driver groaned as they undressed him, twitching and jerking in seeming resistance to the indignity of being forcibly stripped. Pieracki donned his stained olive-green pants. They were stiff and filthy, but they would be warm. He threw his own torn pair into the cab. Von Mecklenburg peeled off the driver's socks with undisguised distaste; his feet were swollen and his toenails had not been cut or washed in weeks. So much for proletarian hygiene, he thought. The count also expropriated—he couldn't resist smiling at the word—the man's thick woolen parka, reluctantly leaving his own Parisian coat behind. Kortschenko ripped the driver's brown shirt down the back and around the sleeves. Then, holding one end of the sweat-drench fabric with his teeth, he wrapped it around his broken hand. Behind the driver's seat they found a half-empty bottle of vodka, an onion, and three pickles. On the floor lay two fur hats and the icons.

"Comrade Vanya lied to Comrade Izya." Von Mecklenburg placed the onion and pickles on the ice.

"Who has the knife?"

"*Voila, mon ami.*"

"May I suggest, gentlemen"—Kortschenko motioned in Golub's direction—"that we eat here discreetly, and alone?"

The men crouched behind the van and silently devoured the food and passed around the vodka. When nothing remained, von Mecklenburg shoved the empty bottle behind the seats and the three wiped their hands and mouths against the snow to eliminate any trace odors. They emerged from behind the cab with crooked expressions on their faces. They were warm, their bellies were full, and the alcohol had gone to their heads.

Golub was sitting on the side of the stream, his legs extended, his head buried in his hands. He appeared to be sleeping. When he heard their approach, he raised his head and looked at them listlessly with bloodshot eyes.

"Ready?" von Mecklenburg said abruptly. "We have no time to lose. The secret police will come looking for us soon."

*

Like inexperienced recruits on their first patrol, the men marched in two wobbly files, avoiding the slippery ice, uncertainly placing their weakened legs on the frozen ground, and cursing when they stumbled over moss-covered rocks, rotting branches, or unexpected hollows. When Kortschenko fell hard on his broken hand, he released an anguished howl; the others just stared, waiting patiently and tiredly for him to climb to his feet and resume walking. Their muscles had atrophied during their confinement, their joints ached from the physical exertion of willing their feet forward in mechanical fashion, their fingers and toes tingled, and their hearts and heads pounded. The sky, formerly a bright blue, had acquired the thick wet cotton-white cloud cover more typical for this time of year. A savage wind raced above them; frigid gusts swooped down shrilly into the ravine and struck their exposed faces with minute particles of hard ice and snow. Their hot sweat mingled with the cold air to produce extended chills along their wet spines.

At one point, Golub looked at the others with supreme indifference.

"I know you ate," he said as he searched their faces for signs of the inevitable cramps. "You reek of alcohol and onions— all of you. You shouldn't have, you know, not after so many days of eating nothing." He spoke clinically, but with what von Mecklenburg decided was a distinct hint of *Schadenfreude*.

"The cramps will come very soon," Golub continued. "They may kill you, you know."

The others ignored his tiresome lecturing and kept on walking. Five minutes later, they chanced upon a bloated corpse lying face up in the ice. It was a girl, no more than fifteen years old, with coal-black hair tied in two braids and a sack-like beige dress made of some coarse material. She was barefoot and her arms lay along her sides, with the palms of her small hands facing upward near the surface of the ice. Her gaunt yellow face had remained well preserved: she had green eyes, long lashes, and what must have at some time been full lips. Only the tip of her nose, which extended above the ice, had begun to rot, creating an unsettling effect that reminded the count of a painting by Kirchner or Dix.

Kortschenko crouched near the girl's body. He could imagine her in a taffeta ballroom gown, descending the marble staircase at the Palais Palffy, twirling on the dance floor, flirting with her white-gloved admirers—and stealing a kiss from him, the young poet who charmed and scandalized the ladies with his energetic recitations from Rimbaud and Baudelaire and, of course, everyone's favorite: Rilke.

"She was so young," he murmured.

"A tragedy, *mon ami*, a tragedy. *I taka piękna*," Pieracki said solemnly. "And so pretty, too."

The men had hardly resumed walking, when the Pole instinctively reached for his stomach and hunched over. He dropped to his knees like a sack of potatoes and began retching. Almost immediately, Kortschenko and von Mecklenburg fell over as well.

Golub resisted a smirk.

"You will live," he said, "but only if we empty your stomachs."

Calmly and methodically, he dropped his knees onto von Mecklenburg's abdomen and shoved two fingers down his throat. The German exploded with vomit just as Golub rolled off. Then he repeated the procedure with Kortschenko and Pieracki. Although his breathing was short and his head throbbed unbearably from the effort, he couldn't resist winking and remarking, as much to himself as to the others: "Boy Scouts." That wasn't quite the truth, but there was no reason to quibble about details in happy circumstances such as these. He was thankful he had learned these techniques in socialist camp, where his teacher, a former Bundist from Vilna who abjured pork but preached Lenin, had insisted that ideological purity was vital, but not enough. For victory to be assured, it was also necessary to shoot and to survive. He had taken the malnourished Yiddish boys with pasty complexions into the mountains and trained them to live off the unyielding land and make do with whatever they hunted, trapped, or gathered. Golub smiled at the thought that the skills he and his comrades had believed were absurdly outdated in the twentieth century had actually proven their worth.

Like shell-shocked soldiers who had just experienced a poison-gas attack, Pieracki, Kortschenko, and von Mecklenburg gasped spasmodically and remained lying on the hard ground, their eyes closed and their faces contorted like terrifying masks. Golub felt completely drained, but he knew he had one more thing to do before they recovered. The communists had had weapons. He patted the bodies and withdrew two revolvers, one from

Kortschenko's pocket, the other from von Mecklenburg's, emptied the chambers, and scattered the bullets among the weeds. Then he struck the firing pins against a rock and flung the guns over opposite sides of the ravine. He searched Pieracki and found a knife and, after inserting it into a crevice between two large stones, snapped the blade. Golub tossed it and the knife handle in the direction of the overturned van. The blade clattered on the ice some ten meters away.

Kortschenko, still dazed, barely mustered a feeble shout.

"What are you doing? What in God's name are you doing?" He had propped himself up on his elbows and spoke from a half-seated position.

"Are you mad?"

"Now you will kill no communists."

"*Durak!* Idiot! Now you will die with the peasants—with the Ukrainians." Kortschenko tried to spit, but could only manage an absurdly curled lip and a dribble of milky saliva.

"With—with your anti-Semites!"

Golub looked at him, his eyes empty, his voice full of indifference.

"Really? Well, then."

*

The men meandered downstream like a band of blind beggars. The violent gusts that periodically blew into and along the ravine swept away some of the dusty snow that covered the treacherous ice. With growing regularity, they encountered variously sized corpses in the stream or on the banks. It was unclear from the positions of the dead bodies whether the peasants had been seeking water or shelter or trying to flee. Those in the ice remained fairly well preserved; the others were in various stages of decomposition, with their clothes creating the jarring impression of material substance where there was, in fact, none. Many lacked shoes; their feet were wrapped in sundry rags bound together with bits of twine and ragged rope and thread. Faded shirts and coats enveloped the bodies in a lifeless mass that blended into the equally colorless environment.

The ravine grew steadily less deep and less steep and, after two hours, they were almost level with the ground around them. The icy wind whipped their eyes, noses, mouths, and cheeks and froze their weakened bodies. Only Golub derived some pleasure from the cooling effect the gusts had on his wounds, but even that sensation rapidly dissipated and his head began to pound like a war drum, as much from the exertion of moving his body as from the merciless cold. His eyes filled with tears and his thoughts, unsurprisingly perhaps, drifted again to the Lower East Side, Yonah Schimmel's delectable kasha knishes, the Third Avenue El, and New York's three baseball teams. And then, as he became increasingly oblivious of his surroundings and began walking in a trance-like state, he started singing, in all likelihood unwittingly, punctuating each line with long breaths and frequent pauses:

> Take me out to the ball game,
> Take me out with the crowd.
> Buy me some peanuts and Cracker Jack,
> I don't care if I never get back,
> Let me root, root, root for the home team,
> If they don't win it's a shame.

Golub froze momentarily and, after raising his left knee a meter above the ground and his right arm high above his head, swung it, as if he were throwing a ball. The others stared at the absurd little American struggling to coordinate his limbs within the confines of his enormous greatcoat.

> For it's one, two, three strikes, you're out,
> At the old ball game.

And then, as suddenly as it had come, the trance was over. Although his arm, leg, and head hurt from the jerky movements, Golub felt a measure of contentment. His world had been shattered, but he realized that, although he had become enmeshed in a series of impossible contradictions, there was, still, a place he could find relief, however fleeting and temporary, from the iron trap that had snapped tight on him.

What he wouldn't give to be at the old ball game at this very moment! His comrades rooted for the underdog Dodgers, but he had always been and would always remain a Yankee fan. Their power, and their ability to get the job done, had impressed him since his first visit to the magnificent stadium in the Bronx that so obviously heralded the inevitable victory of the toiling masses. The Dodgers won by stealth. The Yankees, in contrast, always attacked head-on, like self-confident Bolsheviks who knew that history was on their side. They overwhelmed their opponents. They never compromised. They took advantage of every contradiction. And they never showed mercy—which was the only way to win the pennant or, as Lenin taught, establish the dictatorship of the proletariat.

His wounds began to throb and Golub's mood changed. It was one thing to give up a home run or lose a baseball game, but what was he to do after receiving a blow to the head from representatives of the world proletariat? Was life still possible for a communist?

As Golub resumed walking, Kortschenko placed a crooked finger to his temple and turned to Pieracki: "I told you. The Jew is *meshugge.*"

*

It began snowing after about three hours—a powdery snow at first, followed by swirls of large wet snowflakes, and ending with thick sheets of tiny pellets that struck their faces like little darts. The men could see no more than two meters in front of them and, with the wind and snow driving them inexorably apart, they gathered together and tried to advance as closely as possible. They stuck to the stream, partly because it provided them with a sense of direction and partly because it promised to lead them to some settlement. At one point, either Pieracki or von Mecklenburg suggested they consider some other route, but Golub invoked his scouting experience and insisted they stay on track. No one objected, not because they trusted the American's judgment, but because they didn't trust their own.

Kortschenko's left hand continued to give him no peace. Holding it in his pocket ameliorated the discomfort, but decreased his sense of balance and threatened to send him sprawling to the ground. Keeping the hand exposed to the wind, however, only increased the pain. He tried to distract himself by composing a poem or reciting Rilke, but the pain invariably asserted itself and dragged him back to the prosaic reality. Von Mecklenburg's teeth had become as numb as his face and he did what he had done in similar circumstances during the war: he thought of nothing and concentrated on moving his feet—left, right, left right, left, right—like a Golem. Pieracki's knee tightened after only an hour of walking and he was soon limping. Even that became increasingly difficult when they found themselves on level ground, where the wet snow reached to their knees. Golub's wounds, and the attendant loss of blood, had drained him of both color and energy. Despite his best efforts to keep up, he straggled five meters behind the others, whistling, singing, and humming in a diminishing effort to stay alert.

Except for the howling wind, the incessant pitter-patter of the snow, and their own inaudible groans, the men heard nothing. The funereal sky hung just above their heads like a cracked ceiling, threatening to come crashing down if disturbed by the frailest breeze. Although it was impossible to tell where east and west were, they knew that, unless they found shelter within the next hour or two, they would have to spend a miserable night among the harsh Ukrainian elements.

It was at this time, as their spirits were sinking even more rapidly than before, that they came upon their first hint of a nearby village. With the wind and ice still blinding them, they almost stumbled over some piles of small bodies lying half-buried beneath the snow. The children couldn't have been more than three or four years old. It was highly unlikely, von Mecklenburg coolly suggested, that a gaggle of barely ambulatory *Kinder* could have survived a long trek. They had probably expired soon after they had started their ill-fated journey. Ergo, he concluded, their village could not be far away. His reasoning struck the others as persuasive.

Luck, evidently, was on the men's side. The winds and snow abated for several minutes, just enough time for them to discern the outlines of small peasant huts in the distance to their right. They stopped to make sure their eyes weren't deceiving them and then, after exchanging words of encouragement—somewhat preposterously, Pieracki uttered *"Bon courage, mes amis!"*—they trundled off in that direction. Forward movement became even more onerous than before, as the snowdrifts, rarely less than one meter high, occasionally reached as high as two. Kortschenko kept losing his balance. For Pieracki, every step had become an ordeal. Golub advanced methodically, but with great slowness, like a somnambulist who had strayed from the safety and predictability of his home. Only von Mecklenburg appeared unaffected, trying to create a narrow path for the others by forcing his legs to plow through the heavy snow. It was, he knew, his duty—as a diplomat, as the eldest of the lot, as a soldier, and, of course, as a German.

About half way to the huts their luck ran out. The oppressive silence pressing down on them from all sides came to an abrupt end with what appeared to be gunshots resounding in the distance. They strained to hear above the wind. Golub asked if it might be thunder, but von Mecklenburg noted the regularity and uniformity of the explosions and dismissed the American's suggestion. As he finished speaking, three more shots were fired. The men couldn't tell where the shooters were and what they were firing at, but they naturally assumed they had to be GPU agents hunting them down.

The firing continued—randomly and seemingly without purpose—and the gunshots, now accompanied by shouts, appeared to be coming nearer. It was impossible to tell exactly, as the wind had resumed blowing and the snow swirled about, distorting the sound as well as its direction. It was obvious that they needed to hide. The huts were still one or two hundred meters away. The land was flat on all sides, but to their right there stood what appeared to be a small hill or, possibly, a mound reminiscent of the kind the local population built in honor of their dead heroes.

Von Mecklenburg motioned with his pianist's fingers.

"There. We can hide on the other side of that hillock. We should be safe, at least for now."

*

The mound stood next to twenty or more rows of crooked crosses. Some were almost completely submerged in the snow; others extended to their full height of about one meter. Many consisted of two sticks bound together by a rag or some rope. They were neatly arrayed toward the back, nearer the village, and chaotically distributed and of varying heights farther away.

As the mound loomed before them, they realized that what had at first appeared to be an earthen monument was something entirely different. Speechless, von Mecklenburg could only mutter, "*Das gibt es nicht*—it cannot be." Even in the war, he had not seen anything quite like this. It was a huge pile of corpses, crazily, haphazardly arranged, with limbs and heads poking out grotesquely and bits of rags flapping in the wind, all covered with a thin layer of unevenly accumulated snow.

"There is no more room in the cemetery," he said after

regaining his composure. "Or, perhaps, there is no more strength to dig holes. After all," he sighed, while brushing his right hand over his forehead, "how can the dying bury the dead?"

Pieracki whispered something and froze, to the count's left, while Kortschenko and Golub proceeded to circle the mound, as if hoping to discover traces of living flesh amid the rotting corpses. Wherever they looked, however, they saw dead bodies. Open eyes and open mouths stared back at them with a fish-like indifference and animal ferocity that, literally, took their breath away. When the wind blew, the eyelashes appeared to flutter, hinting at a desire to communicate that made both men shudder.

It was too late to find another place to hide. The shouts were getting closer and, if this was indeed the notorious secret police, there was no time to lose. As the wind grew stronger and the snow began falling heavily again, the four men dove into the bodies. They expected to come into contact with decaying flesh and overpowering smells. Instead, they encountered relatively hard objects, thin, angular, and bony to be sure, but still retaining the texture and suppleness of recently living things. The odor that assaulted their nostrils was not that of decomposition, but of urine, feces, and sweat. The bodies themselves were almost less repulsive to the touch than the sticky, cold, wet rags that encased them.

Although the wind, the snow, the bodies, as well as their own rapidly beating hearts drastically reduced audibility, the men could hear four or five gruff voices, speaking indistinctly in Ukrainian. The voices soon turned to murmurs. Then they fell silent and were replaced by the sound of tugging, pushing, and pulling interspersed with occasional snarls. Pieracki and von Mecklenburg lay completely still. The Pole had sunk into the rotting corpse of what had once been a large man. His rib cage poked him in the stomach and, with every breath he took, Pieracki felt the man's bones creak. Would they break, he thought, and, if they did, would the GPU hear? The German lay atop a small man or boy, still preserved, although consisting almost entirely of skin and bones. The skin was cold and coarse, but as delicate as paper, and it tore every time von Mecklenburg shifted his weight.

"Scavengers," he whispered to Pieracki. "Outside. They are taking bodies."

*

66

Golub and Kortschenko found themselves on both sides of a corpse. They didn't realize at once that it was a woman lying on her back. Her body was thin and hard and there was nothing resembling breasts or hips anymore, but her stringy hair was long and she was clothed in a burlap dress that was as rough as sandpaper to the touch. Her stench was bearable; both men turned their faces toward hers and attempted to control their excited breathing, inhaling and exhaling as steadily and as quietly as they could.

"Stop." It was the woman. "You're tickling me."

"*What?*" Kortschenko almost shouted. "You're alive!"

"*Da,*" the woman replied weakly. "They also collect the living." She released a long sigh and both men winced at the sour smell.

"But this is a graveyard"—Golub had unwittingly taken her bony hand in his—"and you are alive!" To Kortschenko's astonishment, he spoke in Ukrainian.

"*Ukraina kladovyshche,*" she said. "Ukraine is a graveyard. It's time for me to join my children."

What was there to say? How did one speak to a corpse?

"How—how many?" Kortschenko asked timidly.

"Four died. One disappeared."

"What do you mean—disappeared?"

"They eat children."

"Who?"

"Everyone." After a brief silence she went on. "What do you think they're doing out there?"

"It's the GPU," he replied. "They're following us."

"The GPU?" The woman tried to giggle, but produced a noise like a rattle instead. "The villagers are looking for food."

"Living bodies?" Golub interjected.

"Or corpses."

"Will they eat them?" Kortschenko asked. "Are you saying they will eat them?"

"The dead must also live." Then she added: "I am very cold. Breathe on me."

The woman pulled on their arms and drew them closer to her. The three fell silent as they lay entangled amid the bodies, rags, and snow. Outside, the murmuring resumed. It was followed by a shriek and the tugging and pulling ceased. A deep and increasingly

loud groan culminated in a terrible scream and the words, very
definitely in Ukrainian, "Stop! Stop! Good God, stop!" Then there
was a gunshot and the groaning ended. The voices returned to their
murmuring.

"They found someone."

"What will they do now?" Golub asked fearfully.

"Cut him to pieces and fry him. Or her. They say our meat
is better."

"But"—it was Kortschenko again—"but how can you live
like this?"

"Live?"

Neither man dared speak for a few seconds. Kortschenko
felt embarrassed by his naiveté; Golub couldn't believe he was
embracing a dead woman. Marxism had nothing to say about this.
Here, the class struggle had ceased and the dialectic was turned on
its head.

"*A khto Vy?*" Golub asked.

"Kateryna Fedorivna Kha— Khanenko," she answered,
turning her head toward him. "And why are you here, among the
dead, Pan—?"

"Golub. I, I am," he stuttered, "I am an American
journalist."

"But you speak our language!"

"We—we left Kiev after, well—after the pogroms."

"Then why are you here, Pan Golub, hiding among us
corpses?"

Golub's silence was unbearable, almost as unbearable as
the woman's pointed questions, and, hoping to stem his growing
sense of desperation, Kortschenko blurted, "You must have hope,
Kateryna Fedorivna! You will live, you will live! But first you must
have hope!" He realized too late just how absurd he sounded—
again.

She seized Kortschenko's broken hand and pressed it to
the shriveled remains of her bosom. With her other hand she
pulled Golub's face close to hers. He recoiled from the smell of
decay emanating from her mouth, but she held his head tightly.

"We are dead. It is God's will."

Unnerved, Golub stammered, "And—and if there is no—
no God?"

Her response was dismissive.

"No God? Of course there is a God. That is why we suffer. My youngest child was born a cripple—and disappeared. How can you tell me there is no God, Mister Golub? How can you believe such—"

"Kateryna Fedorivna," he begged her, "please be quiet!" Golub squeezed her hand and held it firmly.

"The voices are coming in our direction!"

The woman ignored his entreaties.

"The communists took everything, Pan Golub. Our land, even our cow." Her voice rose. "One cow! We had one cow and the communists took it! And then they took our bread. And when we thought they had taken everything, they took our seeds. The unbelievers destroyed our church and took everything." She appeared to be sobbing.

"Have you ever eaten dead cats, Mister Golub? Or dead horses? Have you ever sifted through manure for seeds? They took our only cow, Mister Golub. They took all the food. They took everything. They—"

"Shhh," Golub pleaded. "You must be quiet—*please*. You must be quiet or they will hear us."

"But I am dead, Pan Golub. What can they do to me?"

"Kateryna Fedorivna, please be quiet. Please—you must lower your voice. Calm yourself. All will be well. But, please, calm yourself—*for God's sake!*"

"No!" she half-shouted. "The dead have nothing to fear."

And then, to both men's horror, she began singing a folk song that Kortschenko vaguely recognized: something about a manipulative woman who invites her lover to a rendezvous, but fails to show up.

> *Ya kazala u vivtorok*
> *potsiluyu raziv sorok,*
> *ty pryyshov mene nema*
> *pidmanula pidvela.*

The murmuring outside appeared to have ended, but she continued loudly with the refrain, which announced the woman's pride at having driven the man out of his mind.

> *Ya zh tebe pidmanula*
> *ya zh tebe pidvela*
> *ya zh tebe molodoho*

z uma z rozumu zvela.

"Kateryna Fedorivna," Kortschenko said, as he placed his right hand over her tremulous lips. "Please, Kateryna Fedorivna, *please* stop. They will hear. *Please* stop."

Golub pressed the woman's head against his chest. Her hair felt like wet straw. She resisted, biting Kortschenko's fingers with her gums and attempting to push Golub away with her tiny fists. Kortschenko placed his left leg over her desiccated abdomen and pushed down hard with his hand. Golub pulled her head toward him with renewed force. The murmuring outside resumed, but it was almost inaudible: the scavengers were probably withdrawing. And then, just as the two men were about to release their hold, they heard a loud snap and the singing ceased.

"What was that?"

"Lord save us," Kortschenko said with unrestrained horror, "we have just killed a corpse!"

Golub's body tightened, his breathing felt constricted, and a stabbing pain, like that produced by a bayonet, rent his gut.

"Oh, my God," he gasped. "I need air! I need air!"

As he surfaced, bits of flesh and bones and rags catapulted away, carried off by the cold wind. He looked about guiltily. The voices were gone. The mound stood quietly in the deep snow. He tried to extricate himself from the corpses, but his foot slipped on an exposed knee bone and he tumbled into the snow. The woman's cold breath seemed to linger on his lips and he scooped up some snow and drank it in. *Her neck had snapped.* That was the horrible sound he had heard. Yes, it was true. Her neck had snapped, because they—*he*—had snapped it. As the realization of what had happened—of the terrible deed that he and Kortschenko had performed—sank in, Golub retched violently. A vile-tasting bile rose to his lips and he spat it out with disgust. Good God! Her neck had snapped and they had killed a dying woman. He retched again on the pristine snow.

Kortschenko tapped him on the back and watched his paroxysms subside. The American stood silently, his lips white, his arms hanging limply at his sides, his head raised, his mouth half-open. The look on his face was one of unalloyed despair. It was as if he, Kortschenko, stood face to face with a corpse. Golub had just escaped the grave, but he still had one foot in it. Or was it both feet? Kortschenko peered into Golub's dark eyes and, except for tears, saw nothing.

"She was going to die anyway. We probably did her a favor."

Golub stared at him and said nothing.

"We ended her suffering."

"And who will end our suffering?"

This time, Kortschenko said nothing.

The wind had abated, but the snow had resumed. It had also grown appreciably darker since the men had arrived at the mound. Once again, the sky was covered with uniformly dirty and impenetrably drab clouds that made it impossible to tell where the sun was and whether it was in fact still suspended from the firmament. The mound appeared to be moving, almost unnoticeably, as if it were breathing, but just enough for their experienced eyes to discern remnants of life. Perhaps because the heavy silence around them felt so oppressive or perhaps because their nerves were so frayed, Kortschenko and Golub thought they heard sinister moans and tell-tale tappings and scratchings. A crow, which had alighted atop the pile, began flapping its wings noisily, disturbing the serenity of the scene and the somberness of their thoughts. It cawed and then flew lazily in the direction of the huts.

*

Pausing every few seconds to listen, Pieracki and von Mecklenburg shoved the limbs, heads, and rags to the side and emerged from beneath the broken bodies. They looked confused, as they blinked and brushed the strands of human hair from their faces. Tiny scraps of yellow skin had attached themselves like autumn leaves to von Mecklenburg's parka and he picked at them with his pianist's fingers. He glanced at the Pole. Pieracki's eyes were wet and red; he was barely breathing and his hands were shaking violently.

"We survived, *mein lieber Freund*," von Mecklenburg said with all the gentleness that his strained condition permitted. "That is what matters."

The four men approached one another. They looked exhausted and shaken and they knew it. Worse, they knew that they would have to follow the scavengers into the village to find shelter for the night. They stood wordlessly in a circle and took deep breaths. Pieracki and von Mecklenburg had lost the fur hats they had taken from the van, but neither appeared to notice or to care.

Kortschenko massaged his aching left hand. Golub's face had turned the color of faded parchment and the dark rings around his lifeless eyes seemed engraved into his features.

As they circled the mound, trying desperately, and failing, to look away, they came upon the spot where the scavengers had gathered. The snow had been flattened by their footsteps and it was stained a dark brown. They espied, half covered in a snowdrift, a battered head attached to a disemboweled torso. The head had once belonged to a young woman, a blonde, with long eyelashes— which might have fluttered in the breeze if they had not been sprinkled with blood—and a long thin nose and tight mouth. The arms, legs, breasts, and buttocks were missing and the abdominal cavity lay open and mangled before them. Two crows were pulling at sinews and picking excitedly at the blue intestines. They flew away after von Mecklenburg waved his hands.

"Cannibals," Golub said, so quietly as to be almost inaudible. "They're not scavengers. They're *cannibals*." He surveyed what remained of the woman's body with glassy eyes. "I think she was still alive. I think they tore her to pieces while she was still alive. I thought I heard groans." He placed one hand on his forehead. "It was *this* woman." He shook his head in disbelief and suppressed a sob.

"They tore her apart while she still lived."

Golub began walking toward the village. He dragged his feet and his head was cocked awkwardly to one side. Von Mecklenburg cast one last look at the bloody mess and followed. There was nothing to be done about it and nothing to be said. He watched the American stagger through the snow. His sudden change in tone—his loss of the combative spirit that had so annoyed everybody—was inexplicable and alarming. Soldiers without the will to live did not. It was as simple as that. Pieracki motioned to Kortschenko and whispered in his ear: "What happened to our communist friend?"

"His fire is gone."

"Yes, I know, but why? He was a fanatic just a minute ago."

"It was extinguished."

"By what? The dead?"

"No, of course not: the living."

"I'm afraid I don't understand," Pieracki insisted. "*We* are

72

the living. He should be glad to be alive. Was it the cannibals?"

"No."

"The dead bodies?"

"Comrade Golub is a native of Ukraine," Kortschenko said.

"I still don't understand, *mon ami.*"

"He has come home. *C'est tout.* That is all."

As Pieracki fell silent, Kortschenko tightened the cloth around his broken hand and strode purposefully after von Mecklenburg. The clever little Pole was too inquisitive. He had managed to deflect his questions for the time being, but Golub's unlikely transformation would keep on raising eyebrows. What could he say? That Golub had just killed a woman? That he and Golub had just killed a woman? That *he* had just killed a woman? Did it matter that she was lying among the dead, in fact, was almost dead? Was killing the almost-dead still killing? Her death was an accident—he knew that—but was it also a crime, even if unintentional? Was the crime greater because she had died in mid-song? It was small wonder that the atheist had begun invoking God. The American Jew obviously couldn't live with himself. The question was: could he?

*

The wind was howling again, like a pack of hungry, wild dogs, whipping the snow in all directions and stinging their tender cheeks, tired eyelids, and dry lips. The sky hung like a heavy, wet, charcoal canopy; they knew that it would be completely dark in no more than half an hour. The men ground ahead unthinkingly, lifting and dropping their legs like pistons in a poorly oiled machine, occasionally stumbling, occasionally falling, frequently pausing to listen to their agitated heartbeats interfere with their labored breathing. Von Mecklenburg led the way, followed by Kortschenko and Pieracki. Golub came last. His head wounds hurt intolerably again, his right lung burned, and he winced with every step. The huts or, more exactly, their dark outlines had become visible, as had an orchard to the left of the village and a well up ahead.

Standing in knee-high snow, von Mecklenburg turned to the others.

"*Vorsicht, meine Herren!*"

Kortschenko and Pieracki approached him, their hands on their knees, their heads bowed as if in prayer, their mouths hungrily ingesting the air.

"We must be very careful now," the count said. "The cannibals probably live in one of those huts." He waved carelessly in their direction.

"Perhaps," Pieracki asked in between breaths, "perhaps I should go ahead?"

"We have no time. Besides, there is strength in numbers."

Kortschenko released a high-pitched yelp.

"*Strength?* What strength? We are impotent, Herr Graf! I say we all go to the nearest hut. If it is empty, we shall live another day. If not, then so be it. Unfortunately"—his voice trailed off with unmistakable bitterness—"we have no weapons." He searched for Golub.

"By the way, *wo ist unser braver amerikanischer Jude?* Our good American Jew was just here."

The Ukrainian found Golub lying face down in the snow some ten paces behind them. His arms were at his sides, his head was buried in the snow, and his legs were as still as logs. Almost miraculously, the banging in his head had stopped as soon as it sank into the snow and a delightful wetness began lapping at his parched mouth. An irresistible warmth—so like the steam in the Russian-Turkish Baths on Tenth Street—seeped into his tired muscles and soothed his overactive mind. He resolved to take advantage of his good luck and keep his eyes shut tightly.

Kortschenko tugged at his coat and heard a groan.

"He's alive. Help me move him. And you, Comrade Golub, wake up. It is time to go. It is too early for you to die. The revolution needs you!"

As Pieracki and Kortschenko turned him over, Golub broke into delirious sobs and pushed them away with his hands.

"Stop!" he implored. "Sleep—I want to sleep. Please let me sleep!"

"*Der ist hysterisch,*" von Mecklenburg declared. "Smack him."

Reluctantly, Kortschenko struck Golub across the face with the palm of his right hand. The sobbing ceased immediately and Golub looked at him with tear-filled eyes. Were they, Kortschenko wondered, also accusatory? But even if they were, what right did the American have to cast accusations at him? They were both either equally guilty or equally innocent. And why in God's name didn't he hit back? Why didn't the proud Jew defend himself? Why was the arrogant Bolshevik incapable of self-assertion? As Kortschenko extended his hand and stroked his wet cheek, Golub turned his face away and whimpered.

*

Kortschenko and Pieracki took Golub by the arms and tried to lead him, his feet dragging in the snow, toward the nearest hut, just visible some twenty meters away. Golub moaned, drifting in and out of consciousness.

"Take him," Kortschenko pleaded with von Mecklenburg. "*Ich kann nicht mehr.*"

The count seized Golub's arm. He had a plan and he knew just how to raise the communist from the dead.

"Come, comrade, move your feet. Help us. Move your feet: one, two, one, two, one, two. Move your feet and you shall soon be sleeping. Perhaps you will dream you are a guest of Iosif Vissarionovich? A banquet at the Kremlin, perhaps? An orchestra and speeches—the applause never ends!—and then a large shiny medal for you, for all that you have done: for your communism, for the Boy Scouts, for this wretched land. Come, comrade, just a few more steps—one, two, one two, one, two, one, two—just a few more steps and we shall all be asleep. And we shall all be dreaming of your Stalin."

Golub's head sank deeper in response, while Pieracki—his breath short and his heart pounding as he strained to carry the American and keep his balance in the snow and wind—was visibly on the verge of collapse. Once again, as so often during his career, it was a question of *jetzt oder nie*. A good general had to change his tactics for the sake of his strategic goals and now was the time to do just that. Von Mecklenburg's voice turned sardonic.

"Or perhaps you will dream of something else, Herr Journalist? Perhaps you will be in Berlin and you will be cheering our little Chancellor? Just think, Herr Journalist, there you are on Unter den Linden, amid the anti-Semitic Prussian masses waving and shouting deliriously, waiting in anticipation, and then the large, black, shiny car glides through the Brandenburg Gate and there, sitting in the back seat, is our beloved Führer—*our* Iosif

Vissarionovich!"

Golub raised his head and opened his eyes.

"*Nein, nein, nein!* Fascists, anti-Semites, barbarians…"

Pieracki and von Mecklenburg released Golub's arms. He stood upright for a moment, took one step forward, and then, with the wind blowing viciously again, tottered and collapsed, his knees buckling under the dead weight of his limp body. The count crouched near Golub's ear.

"*Kommen Sie,* Herr Journalist. You *must* have the strength. The Führer is following us. Can you hear the sound of his tanks? They are coming, Herr Journalist, they are coming."

Von Mecklenburg and Pieracki placed their hands under Golub's arms and yanked him up.

"See?" the count murmured. "He lives. Our little Führer even awakens the masses in this godforsaken country."

Then von Mecklenburg turned to Golub.

"Can you walk, Herr Journalist?" His face resembled that of a soldier on a forced march.

"*Ja.*"

"Just a few more steps."

"Yes, just a few more steps."

"And then we shall be in paradise."

"Yes—in paradise."

"And the angels will sing Hallelujah and Marx and Engels and Lenin will greet us with their long beards and long staffs."

"Yes, just a few more steps and then—in paradise."

*

Kortschenko pushed ahead. It was too cold to stand still and the others did not need his help. He lowered his head like a battering ram and ploughed through the powdery snow, pumping with his right arm, while holding his broken hand against his ribs. He felt a hot sweat on his back and a frenzied thumping in his chest. As he finally caught sight of the hut, he tripped and fell headlong into the snow. His left hand struck something hard and he cried out. It was the remains of a picket fence. He grabbed hold of a tree—its bark had been stripped, probably by ravenous peasants—and leaned his right shoulder against it, waiting for the drumbeat in his chest to subside, listening and squinting, trying to determine if there were any signs of life. He heard nothing. The hut and the yard appeared to be empty. It was possible that the cannibals were waiting inside, sharpening their knives and anticipating their next meal. But—the corners of his mouth curved at the unlikely intrusion of such a banal memory—if he could brave the House of Horrors as a seven year-old at the Wurstelprater, why not this?

The shutters and door had been torn off, perhaps for firewood. The window and door frames were gaping holes, black voids that stared at him like the eyes of a blind beggar on the Naschmarkt. More than half the thatched roof was also missing. It might have blown away or the straw might have been used by desperate peasants to make a thin soup or an inedible gruel. Kortschenko raised high his sluggish feet in order to negotiate the deep snow that had accumulated just before the entrance. Finally, he took a step forward, wobbled briefly as he held his breath and momentarily closed his eyes, and found himself inside. His shirt and coat were soaked through with a sour-smelling sweat and his heart felt close to bursting, a locution he always avoided in his love poetry, but one that seemed appropriate to the occasion now. He stood still and waited. No one attacked. He could hear nothing. He was still alive.

There was, apparently, only one room. A huge object, the clay oven, loomed directly before him, like a sacrificial altar. A table and a bench stood forlornly to his left and what appeared to be a makeshift cot, consisting of a burlap sack presumably filled with straw and draped over a large wooden trunk, to his right. There was no point in looking inside the trunk; it would be empty, its contents stolen, scattered, or eaten. The roof, fortunately, was intact just above the oven. They would be able to rest on top of it. The oven would be cold, but not as cold as the earthen floor. Kortschenko approached the wall to his right and ran the fingers of his good hand along its slippery surface. Snow came down through the hole in the roof, but, except for occasional gusts sliding past the windows or door, there was no wind. He decided to go back for the others.

The cloud cover had acquired an eerie purplish glow and Kortschenko was able to retrace his steps by following the black indentations he had made in the snow. This time, he carefully stepped over the dilapidated fence and turned left. Pieracki and von Mecklenburg were still struggling with the delirious Golub as he approached.

"It is empty," Kortschenko said. "It is no Hofburg, but it will keep us warm."

It took the four men another fifteen minutes to reach the hut. Pieracki and von Mecklenburg led Golub by his arms and, with Kortschenko holding one of his feet, propped him up against the oven. Pieracki then collapsed onto the table like a bale of wet hay, while Kortschenko fell on the bench and released a loud, extended groan. The top of the oven seemed impossibly distant and inaccessible, even to him.

Von Mecklenburg remained standing. The smell of the house was familiar. He had been in huts just like this one in 1918, when they had been requisitioning swine and eggs and wheat from the peasantry. The Ukrainians had fought back, forming armed bands with scythes and pitchforks and ancient revolvers. They had been slaughtered, of course—what else were the soldiers to do?— swiftly, effortlessly, and efficiently. Small wonder that the peasants had cheered wildly as the German forces withdrew in disgrace after the ignominious collapse of the Reich. This time, there was no one to fight, no one to expropriate, and no one to cheer. And there was nothing to expropriate. The land, so bountiful that it could feed the German and Austrian armies even in wartime, was as empty and barren and cold as this house.

He began rummaging through the pockets of the parka he had expropriated—he knew that the word described perfectly his shameful act—from the unfortunate driver. The left pocket was empty, but the right one contained a small box of wooden matches and a notebook. He flipped through the greasy, dog-eared pages. When he turned them toward the hole in the roof, he could just discern what appeared to be columns of numbers, dates, place names, and ruble amounts. The driver had been almost Germanic in his attention to detail in what was, in all likelihood, a ledger of his work and pay as a transporter of prisoners.

Von Mecklenburg shook Pieracki, who lay with his dead legs dangling over the side of the table.

"Look into your pockets. I found matches. Perhaps you have something, too."

Pieracki growled. Without rising from the table, he fished out a bread crust and a small tin and handed them to von Mecklenburg. The count opened the tin and smelled the contents.

"Gentlemen," he announced triumphantly, "we have

dinner and we have tobacco."

No one responded.

*

Von Mecklenburg lowered his heavy body onto the bench and, after propping his elbows on his trembling knees, dropped his burning face into his hands. They were rough and calloused and they smelled. They had once been the hands of a Prussian aristocrat. Now they had become the hands of the world proletariat.

"*Danke*, Herr Graf," a voice said weakly from the direction of the oven. It was Golub.

"Your methods are unique, but you saved my life. I am not sure it was worth saving, but thank you nonetheless. Tell me: Do you have a cigarette?"

"Only tobacco."

"But you have matches?"

"*Jawohl.*"

"And paper?"

"A notebook of some kind."

"Then we are in luck," Golub said hoarsely. "Could you come here—to me? I cannot move."

"I shall try, Herr Journalist, I shall certainly try."

Von Mecklenburg raised his leaden head, planted his hands on the bench, and lifted himself up with a deep groan. The tiredness had sunk into his bones and he found it almost impossible to move his feet. For a moment he appeared to sway, to be on the verge of falling, but he managed to grab the table with his right hand just in time. Then, slowly—almost as slowly as when he was walking through the waist-high snow—von Mecklenburg willed himself to move in the direction of Golub's emaciated voice.

"Please sit down, Herr Graf. You are standing just above me."

Von Mecklenburg dropped down like a sack of grain.

"*Vorsicht*, Herr Graf, please be careful. The floor is hard. Give me the tobacco and the paper—*bitte*. I suspect you have had less experience than me with rolling cigarettes."

As he handed him the notebook and the tin, von Mecklenburg looked closely at Golub. He could see only a shadow slouched against the oven.

"*Ich verstehe Sie nicht*, Herr Journalist. I do not understand you. You are a militant communist and yet, now, you speak to me like a gentleman—or a Boy Scout."

Golub tore a page from the notebook and licked it. Then he opened the tin, placed it carefully on his stomach, took a large pinch of tobacco, and proceeded to roll it into a rough approximation of a cigarette.

"*Sie haben Feuer?*"

Von Mecklenburg fished out the box from his coat pocket and, with unsteady fingers, succeeded in lighting a match after four tries. The hut was suddenly bathed in a dancing bluish light and both men could clearly glimpse Pieracki lying on the table, hands beneath his head, with one leg touching the floor, and Kortschenko sprawled out on the bench. The tobacco caught fire just as the flame went out. Golub inhaled, producing a bright orange glow at the tip. As he coughed, he handed the makeshift cigarette to the count.

"This is," Golub cleared his throat, "by far the worst tobacco I have ever smoked."

Von Mecklenburg dragged on it and choked as well.

"Yes," he said, "but I have never tasted a better cigarette."

How rapidly one adapts to inhuman conditions, he thought. Indeed, how rapidly one becomes a savage, if savagery is all there is. He recalled the bloody torso in the snow. The cannibals were brutes, but what would he have done in their place? *Nein, es war unmöglich.* The count banished the thought. There was no point in dwelling on the impossible, except, perhaps, to acknowledge that, however impossible, it might just be possible.

The paper burned quickly and the men remained silent until they consumed the cigarette. The nicotine went to their heads, producing a state of mild exaltation and dulling the gnawing pain in their stomachs. Von Mecklenburg leaned against the oven and wrapped himself tightly in his parka.

"We used to smoke in the trenches," he said, "to kill the hunger. But, even then, our tobacco was better than this. Of course, we had to be very, very careful. The snipers were always watching and I saw eight *Kameraden* get bullets in their heads. There was one instance, in particular, that—"

"Excuse me, Herr Graf," Golub interrupted, "but there is something I must ask you." He hesitated before continuing.

"Are you a Nazi? I must know. I do not think I will
survive this ordeal and I want to know who my companions in
death are."

"Would it matter if I were?"

"I could not have shared this cigarette with you."

"Then rest assured that I am not. The National Socialists
are hooligans and their leader is a foolish man. I am not one of
them. Indeed, like my good friends Jünger and von Salomon, I
never could be, as much from temperament as from conviction.
But I shall be frank with you, Herr Golub. These gangsters may do
us some good. We Germans have become soft, decadent—tired.
Our democrats are useless and our conservatives are ignorant. We
dance and prance and debate and the country is going to hell.

"Do you understand me, Herr Golub? We who had no
right to fail have failed. *Deutschland ist bankrott und kaputt.* And even
now the aristocrats—people such as I—we twiddle our thumbs
and drink champagne. So this Hitler and his brownshirts—they will
shock us awake. They will force us to save the Fatherland."

"That is what you hope, Herr Graf."

"My family—we are diplomats, for three generations,
going back to Bismarck. We serve Germany, Herr Golub. But the
socialists, the communists, and—I beg your pardon—the Jews,
they serve other masters. But not Deutschland, not my
Fatherland."

"You are, I see, an anti-Semite."

"Only slightly," von Mecklenburg responded, "only very,
very slightly and mostly as a matter of taste. In reality, I am a friend
of the Jews. It is Herr Hitler who is your enemy. Not I. Not the
true servants of Germany."

Golub tried peering into the count's eyes, but all he could
see was the dark outline of his head.

"Do you know why I became a communist, Herr Graf?
Yes, obviously, I found the ideal attractive. And this country is,
despite all its"—Golub appeared to search for a word—
"*shortcomings,* still a beacon of hope for the working people of the
world. Perhaps not for you, but for those who toil with their hands.
But that is not the reason. Do you know what is, Herr Graf? May I
be honest with you? I wanted to stop being a Jew. It is that simple.
I was tired of this impossible race. I wanted to be nobody,
anybody—*anybody* but a Jew. And communism promised me an

answer to this infernal Jewish question. It let me be a Bolshevik. It let me be strong and build the future with my own hands. It let me abandon this terrible obsession with a glorious past that existed thousands of years ago. It let me leave the ghetto and the desert.

"The freedom, Herr Graf, the freedom! You cannot imagine the freedom!"

Von Mecklenburg was astonished by Golub's outburst of sincerity and said nothing. Then he nodded knowingly. He had heard Germans speak the same way just after the war had ended and the Kaiser, who had no right to abandon his people, had abdicated. They sought freedom in Berlin's cabarets and bordellos. They tried to forget who they were. They tried to forget Goethe, Lessing, Beethoven, Wagner, and Heine. And they had failed, inevitably and necessarily. And when the little man promised them salvation, they flocked to him—like sheep. The moral was as simple as it was obvious: You could never outrun your own shadow and, if you tried, you always fell flat on your face.

"But you are still a Jew, Herr Golub. And you always will be a Jew. Just as I am and will always remain a German. My family owns thousands of hectares of land, Herr Golub. We grow wheat and rye and we feed what you would call the Prussian war machine. We live on a large estate. I have stables, horses, servants. I am a perfect nobleman, a landowner *par excellence*, a member of your hated upper class. I speak French and English and I have relatives in the aristocracies of those countries. As you know, I buy my clothes from Parisian houses. But I cannot stop being a German, Herr Golub, even when I eat boiled beef at the Savoy or escargots at Maxim's. Besides, look around you. These people welcomed communism. Indeed, I wager those cannibals were once Party activists! And communism is now destroying them, just as"— suddenly von Mecklenburg felt very tired—"just as it will destroy you. I beg your pardon, Herr Golub: just as it *has* destroyed you. Excuse my garrulous nature"—the count had already closed his eyes and could barely enunciate the words—"but I must rest."

Golub looked at the large man sitting next to him, his chin resting on his chest, and sleeping. He was breathing regularly, almost peacefully. The German was his class and racial enemy, he was a militarist and a pompous buffoon, but he could also talk sense, just like a worker. Had their conversation lasted a while longer, perhaps he, Golub, would have confessed what he had done. There was no God, of course, and there was no sin, certainly no sin that transcended class and class conflict, but his senseless killing—or was it murder?—of the dead woman was as close to being a pure sin as he could imagine.

Abstract moralizing threatened to make him lose touch with reality and Golub instinctively recoiled from his thoughts. On the other hand, what difference did abstractions make, now that he had actually killed a dead woman? He recalled the snap of her neck—the muffled sound that had such portentous consequences—and felt sick. Amazingly, he even smelled the stench of her breath again. He sniffed the air around him. No, this was for real. Someone was breathing at him from the oven above. He could feel it distinctly.

"Who's there?" he cried in Ukrainian. "*Khto tam?*"

There was no response, not even a sound. It could have been a corpse, a rotting *baba*, the odor of whose dead body had wafted downward with a breeze. Or it could have been another near-dead woman motioning to him desperately for help. He knew the dead could not communicate, but perhaps the near-dead could? Or perhaps she was shaking her fist at him, threatening to take revenge on the killer Jew? Or was she urging him to join her on the oven? To abandon the living and all their ridiculous plans, schemes, and hopes and find peace by entering the timeless realm of the dead?

Golub pressed his spine against the oven. It was comforting to feel the hardness of the cold clay against his hair. His head hurt and his limbs were numb. He felt very cold and very weak. He unbuttoned the coat and slipped his head inside. His breathing had become rapid and shallow and he noticed that, strangely, he was inhaling through his mouth and exhaling through his nose. His stomach and lung and legs hurt and his head was spinning, but at least his wounds no longer bled. Perhaps he really would dream tonight: of the Catskills, of Orchard Street, of Schimmel's knishes, of the New York Yankees, of the City College, of the debates with the detestable Trotskyites, of the delicious pickles on Essex, of the corned beef with mustard on rye at Katz's, of the sweet wines at Seder. Did God exist? Would the Messiah ever come? Was Stalin really a genius? What would he tell his father when he came home? There were too many questions and they were all unanswerable. He would have to have a good breakfast tomorrow—three scrambled eggs with five strips of bacon and heavily buttered toast and a cup of black coffee—and maybe then he would see things clearly.

*

Dawn found the men feeling as physically drained as the day before. Half-somnolent, Kortschenko rotated his head, first to the left, then to the right, hoping to revive the circulation and relax his rock-hard neck muscles. His broken hand had swollen to what felt like twice its usual size and he noticed that even bending his fingers had become a strenuous undertaking. He began massaging them tenderly with his right hand, pulling delicately, raising them, and trying to make a fist. Both his hands were as black as a coal-miner's. The dirt had embedded itself in his pores and would require repeated rubbings with pumice to expunge. He ran his good hand over his chest and ribs and stomach. The fat was gone, the muscles had turned flabby, and the bones trembled just below his skin. And he smelled. It was a vile, putrid smell, the kind one encountered amid the refuse behind the cheap restaurants and *Beiseln* in working-class Vienna: of fresh excrement and rancid sweat, his own as well as those of the corpses around him. He smelled just like the country he had vowed to serve, defend, and protect when he had unthinkingly agreed to join the Organization over a glass of a very fine Burgenländer at the Café Central.

Pieracki lifted his inert right leg onto the table and carefully examined the knee with his hands. It didn't appear to be broken, but yesterday's forced march had made it as useless as a dull knife. He lowered his right foot to the ground and tried standing. His knee buckled and a sharp bolt shot up his leg to his hip and spine. Another three equally awkward attempts followed and Pieracki saw that, if he kept his knee locked and his leg perfectly straight, it could sustain his weight for a few seconds. Still, he would, even in the best of circumstances, have to refrain from using his leg for several days. But how could he rest—and how could his leg recover—without food? It was a vicious circle and there seemed to be no escape from it. Fortunately, his stomach had long since stopped growling, having shrunk in on itself and settled into a permanent ache, like that of a bad tooth.

Von Mecklenburg opened his eyes with his head resting on Golub's shoulder and his knees tilted leftward against Golub's outstretched legs. Unlike his gut, his mouth, while sore and inflamed, no longer hurt. He looked closely at Golub. His eyes were shut and a tiny bubble hung precariously from the tip of his nose. It was obvious that he was not, as they had once suspected, an informer. Nor was his communism more than skin-deep. It was confined to bombastic rhetoric and rooted in the spiritual perturbations of his divided self and deeply troubled soul. He talked like a Bolshevik, but he could never act like one. He was too weak, too irresolute for that. No genuine Bolshevik with an unflinching belief in the infallibility of the Party and the rightness of his cause would have thought twice about being berated and beaten by his comrades. Whatever happened belonged to the past and, in the final analysis, did not matter. It *could not* matter for a real Bolshevik, because the only things that really mattered were the class struggle, the proletariat, the Party, and the revolution.

It was obvious that the reason for his weakness was that Golub remained, despite his feverish efforts to become a non-Jew, the quintessential Jew. He knew too much, he felt too much, and he thought too much to be a Bolshevik. The contradictions were unsustainable and certainly accounted for Golub's infuriating combination of aggressiveness, arrogance, passivity, wisdom, stupidity, and naiveté. Alas, these contradictions made him no less dangerous. After all, you knew where you stood with the outright bandits, such as Herr Hitler, or the fanatics, such as Comrade Stalin. But where did you stand with the thousands of flag-waving marchers who believed or, just as possibly, did not? Perhaps there still was hope for the American. Two more days in this hell, von Mecklenburg thought, and he may even become a fascist.

"Come, Herr Golub, it is time to wake up."

Von Mecklenburg examined his face more closely. The bubble was immobile and he appeared not to be breathing. The count placed his hand beneath his nostrils and felt nothing. He placed it on his heart and also felt nothing. Then he took Golub's hand and put two fingers on his pulse. Again, there was nothing.

"Comrade Golub," he announced to the others, "appears to have left us for a better world."

"*Vous êtes certain?*" Pieracki said.

"How odd, but I think he was coming to his senses. This, all this"—von Mecklenburg opened wide his eyes—"appears to have brought him back to a semblance of reality."

The count had given him an opening and Kortschenko jumped at it.

"*Eigentlich*," he explained, "actually—well, actually, it is much simpler than that. It was the mound, in the graveyard. We were lying there and—how can I put this?—well, I must warn you that this will shock you. Golub killed one of the corpses. He—"

"He killed a *dead* woman?" Pieracki looked at Kortschenko with large, incredulous eyes.

"Yes, he held his hand against her mouth."

"But how could he kill a dead woman?"

Kortschenko was sitting on the bench by now.

"She was alive, *eigentlich*, and she was talking very loudly—*too* loudly. She even began singing. We pleaded with her to stop, but she wouldn't." He spoke rapidly, nervously, and his heart was racing.

"You see, the cannibals might have heard her."

"I heard nothing," von Mecklenburg countered. "You were—"

"Neither did I," said Pieracki.

"—afraid. The half-dead cannot speak loudly. I know that from the war, *meine Herren*. She was probably whispering, but your fear and overactive imagination magnified the volume."

"It was Golub who thought she was shouting," Kortschenko promptly corrected him. "I only heard her whisper. I would've stopped him if I'd known what he intended to do."

"But surely it was an accident," von Mecklenburg insisted. "Surely he did not intend to kill her."

"No, no, of course not. I expressed myself badly, Herr Graf. Forgive me. The poor man! I would've stopped him if I'd only known. But how could I have known? I couldn't see. It was dark, very dark. And the smell! It was terrible. But you know, of course. I could only hear very, very little. And then she began shouting and singing and both of us feared that the cannibals would find us, so we—I mean, Golub—covered her mouth with his hand—I couldn't, my hand is broken, as you know—and he must have pressed hard, *too* hard, and then all I remember is hearing a slight snap, a very slight snap, and then she stopped. And I knew, and he knew, that he had made that snap. He had snapped her neck—and she stopped singing. It was an accident, of course, but it shocked him nonetheless. It shocked me, too, of course."

Pieracki observed Kortschenko carefully. His ramblings were too disjointed and too agitated to be fully sincere. The Ukrainian was obviously trying to conceal something—some important detail, perhaps about the Jew, perhaps about himself. And why was he trying to conceal it? His curiosity had been piqued—what would Sherlock Holmes do in such circumstances?—but there was no reason to pursue that line of enquiry just now. The questions could wait.

"What shall we do with the body?" the Pole asked.

"What *can* we do?" von Mecklenburg replied. "It belongs outside. There, at least, it will not rot before our eyes."

"But the cannibals!" Kortschenko cried. He eyed the others apprehensively and ran his hands through his unkempt hair.

"We cannot let the cannibals—"

"Compose yourself, my young friend," the count said quietly. "We will submerge it in the snow. May the poor devil rest in peace. Perhaps you can compose a poem? A tribute to our fallen *Kamerad*?"

Pieracki lowered his legs and grimaced.

"And then we must find something to eat." His legs touched the ground.

"And I need a splint for my knee. I can barely walk."

Von Mecklenburg extracted the thin bread crust from his pocket and broke it into three pieces the size of Communion wafers.

"*Bon appétit, meine Herren*: here is our breakfast. As to your knee, my young Polish friend, you can bind it with Golub's shirt. It will be a *memento mori*. What should we do with his coat? Keep it?"

"*Nein, nein*," Kortschenko muttered. "It's too big and it smells. Bury him in it."

*

The cloudless sky was an astonishingly bright cerulean blue. The air remained bitterly cold, but the sun shone unsparingly and, as the men stepped outside, they instinctively raised their faces to its warmth and light. Kortschenko even spread his arms and a small curve appeared on his lips. Seven crows were sitting on the thatched roofs, some pecking in the snow, some turning their heads from side to side. Pieracki snapped off two dry branches from a nearby apple tree, broke them in two, and tied the four pieces to his knee with Golub's shirt. He shook from the strain and waited for the blackness to fade before remarking, "A crow would be good."

"You will never catch it," the count said with a hint of exasperation. "But there may be a potato or two somewhere in the garden. The peasants find all manner of vegetables throughout the year on my estate."

The three men trudged wearily to the back of the hut. Up to one meter of snow hid the garden and only the jagged tops of some bushes and small fruit trees were visible. Beyond a pleated fence there stretched a long and gently undulating expanse of silver snow that rose into the distance and was punctuated by bluish indentations on an otherwise glassy surface. A red tractor stood, tilted and soundless, at the summit of the hill, apparently abandoned by the peasants and forgotten by the authorities. Von Mecklenburg surveyed the terrain ruefully. Even if he knew where the potatoes had been planted, it would be impossible to dig in the frozen ground.

"Look over there." Pieracki pointed to a small furry creature lying near the outer wall of the hut. "What is it?"

"A squirrel, I think," Kortschenko said. "Yes, it's a dead squirrel."

"Frozen?"

"Looks like it."

"Is it rotten?"

"No, it looks fresh."

"Do you see any worms?"

"No. It looks fresh. But it's probably frozen."

"It'll have to thaw, I suppose."

Von Mecklenburg's face lit up.

"Have you forgotten, *meine Herren?* We have matches!" He rubbed his hands with anticipation.

"Today we shall dine—"

"—like kings?" The old Prussian was being ridiculous again, but Pieracki knew better than to grin at a moment like this.

Kortschenko gingerly raised the squirrel by its tail, brought the dead animal to his nose, and smelled it. There was no odor. He examined the fur. It appeared to be full. It was unclear whether the creature had died and then frozen or simply frozen while seeking shelter from a storm. He had often encountered dead animals while

88

hiking in the Wienerwald, but it would never have occurred to him to regard them as fit for a meal. Kortschenko smelled the squirrel again, just to make sure. But the circumstances had changed, hadn't they? The brutality was all-pervasive and he, too, was adapting to it. After all, what choice did he have? Was there any alternative to becoming a brute? Apparently not. Would he, after he returned home, still remember how to eat a *Nusstorte* at Demel's without embarrassing himself?

"Leave it in the sunlight," Pieracki advised. "It'll thaw a bit. And you, Herr Graf, you and I will make a fire fit for royalty."

*

An ominous cloud cover had swept back in like a huge wave and the wind had resumed blowing. Large snowflakes had begun falling, fluttering like gay butterflies against the backdrop of the gloomy sky. Golub's body lay in the snowdrift to the left of the entrance. Were it not for the impression it made while sinking to the ground, no trace of him would have remained. Kortschenko looked thoughtfully at the spot where he was buried. Shouldn't they say something over his grave? In Vienna, first they held a solemn service at St. Barbara's and then they transported your coffin, festooned with flowers and wreaths, from the Postgasse to the Zentralfriedhof. Here, they—*we*—just dumped you in the snow. He crossed himself and bowed his head. Silently, von Mecklenburg and Pieracki filed past him into the hut.

They scrutinized the room in which they had spent the night. There was the table, the two benches, and nothing else beside a badly chipped and moldy icon of Christ the Pantocrator hanging crookedly to their right. Coarsely hewn gouges and holes disfigured all the walls, usually near the base. One of the holes was particularly deep and had probably served as a hiding place for flour, grain, or potatoes. They knew that Communist Party activists searched for foodstuffs in the walls, in the floor, and in the garden, using long iron rods to poke for hollow spaces that supposedly concealed vast caches of illicit kulak provisions. The inhabitants of this hut either had much food stored away or, more likely, had been the targets of repeated requisitions. Either way, they had to have been deemed filthy kulaks and were either deported or starved or hounded to death. Whatever food there was had obviously been confiscated and the ubiquitous vermin had probably devoured the stray kernels that escaped the ideological zeal of the Bolsheviks.

Von Mecklenburg approached the large clay oven that stood, icy to the touch, in a corner of the hut. Some kind of bundle, perhaps a pile of rags, lay on top. As the others watched, he placed one knee on a small embankment and raised the other slowly, less from caution as from weakness. His heart beat rapidly—it had never been quite this difficult to perform such a simple physical act—and his bony knees hurt from the hard clay. He stood upright, steadied himself, and, after repeating the procedure and waiting for the hammering in his head to ebb, climbed to the top of the oven and lay face down on his stomach. The bundle was now within easy reach. He extended his hand and tugged at the rags. Something rustled and a mouse dashed out, causing him to jerk his hand back.

"*Eine Maus!*" he shouted. "Catch it!"

The rodent leaped off the oven in a gentle arc and landed on the floor near Pieracki's feet. Caught off guard by the sudden commotion, the Pole lost his balance and, arms flailing about like a windmill, fell on his back. Kortschenko stood helplessly and swore, as his eyes darted about the room. The mouse had vanished. He extended his good hand to Pieracki, who grabbed it and struggled to get back on his feet. By the time he was standing again, both he and Kortschenko were sweating profusely. The Ukrainian was considering the appropriate expletive for the absurdity of their situation, when he gasped with astonishment.

"*Das gibt es nicht!*"

"What? What can't be?"

"*Die Maus.*" The Ukrainian pointed at the floor. "You fell on it. It's dead—*there*, right there, where you fell. You fell on it and killed it."

"Dessert," Pieracki grinned while rubbing the back of his head. "Our luck must be changing."

"Surely you must be joking."

"But why, *mon ami?*"

"It's a mouse! We can't eat a mouse!"

"*Pourqouis pas, mon ami?*" Pieracki replied. "At least it's not a rat. Back in the jail, we dined on a rat, did we not, Herr Graf? And it was a very good rat, indeed, as I recall."

"But it's a rodent!" Kortschenko protested. "It's vermin. One cannot eat vermin!"

"It is food," Pieracki stated, surprised at his own insouciance.

Von Mecklenburg watched the two young men with amusement. He hadn't expected the Pole to be this pragmatic and the Ukrainian to be this fastidious. He recalled how Pieracki had retched the day after they had devoured the rat and here he was, the very same boy-man, playing the role of the battle-hardened veteran! Had he changed or had he always been like this? In all likelihood, the young Pole hailed from some backward province that had historically lain outside the core of Poland's royal traditions and genteel manners, perhaps the Masurian Lakes region or Volhynia. In contrast, the same Ukrainian who had regarded the driver with cold-blooded indifference and had done nothing to prevent Golub from killing the woman was now playing the excessively refined aristocrat who kissed hands and swooned cloyingly. Despite his best efforts to be a hardened revolutionary, the young Viennese poet was just that: a young Viennese poet. And Vienna, obviously, was where he belonged.

Satisfied with his perspicacity, the count returned to the bundle. He poked it with his forefinger, but no second mouse emerged. He took hold of a corner of coarse burlap and pulled it toward himself. The bundle was a body or, more exactly, a skeleton wrapped in smelly rags. The hair was white and short and curled, probably belonging to an old woman. The *babas*, he recalled from his time in Ukraine, loved to recline atop the ovens, where they could stay warm and keep out of the younger people's way. This one had probably starved and, with no one to dispose of her, had remained hidden from sight. Even the cannibals had failed to find her. Only a few strands of flesh remained attached to her skull. The area around the nose and cheeks still retained some vaguely human features, but whatever benign effect they produced was negated by the striking whiteness, and unintentional savagery, of her perfectly straight and healthy teeth.

A small, black, leather-bound prayer book, with a gold cross embossed on its front, lay on her chest. He considered taking it for the fire, but decided that his desperation was not yet great enough to warrant sacrilege. He sighed heavily and replaced the burlap covering. Perhaps he, too, should consider praying? It did not save the dead woman from extinction, but who was to say it made no difference? Perhaps her death was painless, even welcome, as she prepared herself for an encounter with her Maker? And how did the atheist Golub die? Was he angry at the unfairness of existence or reconciled with his sad fate? Or, just as possibly—perhaps even more probably—was he despondent, despairing, and without any hopes, expectations, or illusions to sustain him? Was that why he expired in the dead of night, completely and terrifyingly alone? Was that why he fell impelled to seek his, von Mecklenburg's, camaraderie over a cigarette? How desperate must he have been to extend a hand to his mortal enemy!

"What did you find?" Kortschenko asked.

"*Nichts. Eine alte tote Frau.*"

"Should we bury her outside?"

"I think she is quite comfortable where she is. Let her rest in peace. She will do us no harm here."

*

Von Mecklenburg was exhausted and wanted only to lie down, to sleep, to embrace oblivion, but he knew that the worst thing one could do in the face of overwhelming hopelessness was to embrace it. He had seen what that led to on the front. However difficult things became, one had to soldier on, to keep busy, to go about doing whatever one had to do, however trivial, however unimportant, however absurd. Even something as simple as shaving, as sliding the razor along one's cheek as one tried to catch a glimpse of oneself in a jagged piece of mirror and, for the thousandth time, resisted the temptation to slice one's throat, gave trench life an ephemeral, though not entirely insignificant, meaning. He bent over, gently grasped the handle, and opened the little iron door to the stove. It was hard to see inside, but he thought he could make out the charred remains of some wood. He touched it to see if it was dry. It was. He then motioned to the others.

"Bring me the twigs. I think I can get a fire going. And go see if the squirrel has thawed—*bitte*."

The Ukrainian had placed the squirrel in the sun, cradled between two low-lying branches of the apple tree. He went outside to retrieve it and, after shooing away two hungry crows, brought it back, a smile on his face.

"It is softer, still frozen, but softer," he said. "Should I smack it? I have never done this, you know. Should I smack it?"

"Skin it."

"If you recall, Herr Graf, our beloved comrade threw the knife away."

"Use this." Von Mecklenburg handed him the tobacco tin. "Take the cover and sharpen the side. Here—on the oven."

Twenty quick strokes later, Kortschenko felt the edge: it was sharp enough to serve as a makeshift knife. The Pole, meanwhile, had massaged the squirrel with his thumbs and then took it by its tail and slammed it, violently and in rapid succession, against the wall. The skull cracked—the sound made the Ukrainian unwittingly think of Kateryna Fedorivna—while the flesh became supple and the skin appeared to loosen. Pieracki dropped the bloody carcass on the table. Feeling nauseous, Kortschenko struggled to make an incision just below the neck. The tin was too dull for a clean cut, but persistent rubbing finally produced a tear. He pulled at the skin, while cutting the membranes that held it to the flesh. Pieracki took hold of the squirrel's head and tugged sharply at the skin. It detached from the flesh with surprising ease. The two men repeated the procedure on the other side of the squirrel. Half an hour later, the mangled pink body lay on the table, surrounded by flakes of slimy skin and wet hair.

Von Mecklenburg had succeeded in starting a small fire on the remnants of a half-burned log. He kept the dancing yellow flame alive by feeding it tiny twigs and bits of dry rags.

"Did you remove the guts?" he asked. "You have to remove the guts. *Schnell, bitte.* This fire will not last long."

Pieracki held the squirrel, while Kortschenko, by now almost expertly, like a field surgeon, slid the tin down the breast to its groin. Although half-frozen, the flesh opened easily to reveal the innards: a gleaming mass of pink and red and brown organs.

"The honor is yours," he said with disgust. He felt the bitter taste of bile in his mouth and swallowed loudly. The taste remained and he puckered his lips and spat.

"But then you will skin the mouse," Pieracki informed him. "*Quid pro quo, mon ami, quid pro quo.*"

Von Mecklenburg grabbed the squirrel and held it above the flame with one hand, while feeding the fire with the other. The meat began to crackle. He slid the squirrel over the fire, turned it over, and, when the outside appeared to have cooked, opened it and placed the inside over the flame. The fire sputtered and von Mecklenburg motioned to Pieracki to blow on it.

"And the mouse? *Wo ist die Maus?*" the German asked impatiently. "Prepare the mouse. We shall soon be ready and we will not have much time before the fire goes out."

When he was finished, Kortschenko shoved the red thing into von Mecklenburg's waiting hands and hurried outside, where he retched until his gut cramped up with pain. When his stomach muscles relaxed, he sank both hands into the snow and washed off the blood and vomit and bile. To his horror he realized he was performing his ablutions in the very spot where Golub lay.

"Oh, my God!" he cried.

He crossed himself. This was an abomination, a violation of the sanctity of the dead. Had he sunk to the level of the atheist Bolsheviks? Kortschenko felt nauseous again and retched, ejecting a thin trail of yellow and brown bile onto the snow. A tight knot formed in his abdomen and remained there even after he rose to his feet and crossed himself again.

When he staggered back into the hut, the squirrel and the mouse lay on the table. Kortschenko eyed them suspiciously. His first inclination was to run outside and empty his gut, but the others were inviting him to join them on the bench. Kortschenko sat on the left, with von Mecklenburg in the middle and Pieracki on the right. They stared at their meal, silent and pensive, as if they were having second thoughts. The squirrel was black and brown and pink from the irregular application of the fire. The mouse was cooked only in spots. The fire had gone out before it was done and both von Mecklenburg and Pieracki had known, after looking at each other inquisitively, that they lacked the strength to light another one. Kortschenko observed the carcasses skeptically, sensing that he was about to abandon his life as a civilized inhabitant of the world's most civilized city. He was on the verge of becoming a barbarian and there would be no going back.

"Come"—Pieracki broke the spell—"let us eat. Wait: Should we pray first?"

The count took the squirrel in his hands and tore off bits of flesh, placing them in four neat piles, three small and one large.

"The small piles are for now. The large one we divide in the morning. *D'accord?* And eat slowly, *meine Herren*, eat very, very slowly. Or we shall join Comrade Golub beneath the snow."

*

94

They had eaten little and they had followed von Mecklenburg's admonition to eat slowly, but their empty stomachs had rebelled immediately against the sudden intrusion of solids and the piercing pinpricks that assaulted all parts of their guts struck each of them simultaneously. The three men lay on the hard earthen floor, holding their stomachs tightly and writhing in pain, unable to ease the anguish, to make the cramps subside, to return their guts to the familiar hollowness to which they had become accustomed and which now promised salvation.

"Remember what the Jew did!"

Pieracki plunged two fingers into his throat and his gut expelled a clump of red meat and some olive-green liquid. His body contorted and there followed a series of tremendous heaves. The rest of the squirrel lay in a puddle of slime and phlegm on the floor beside him. He curled up, too weak to move and too weak to speak, panting desperately, like a dog that had just been beaten. After Kortschenko and von Mecklenburg were done, their three wilted bodies rested on the cold packed earth, drained of all energy, of all feeling and strength, to the point of lacking corporeal substance. They said nothing—indeed, they had no strength to speak—only moaning and running their hands along their abdomens, very carefully, very, very delicately, almost as if they were caressing a child's head or, it occurred to Pieracki just before he drifted into sleep, a woman's breast.

A familiar scratching and rustling awoke Kortschenko. Five crows had flown into the hut and were feasting on the rodents. Two were fighting over a morsel, flapping their wings and pecking at each other. The others flew in and out with bits of meat in their beaks. He tried to scare them away, but his throat was dry and he managed only a whimper. The crows looked at him momentarily, as if in dismay, and then resumed their frenetic pecking.

"Let them have it," he heard von Mecklenburg say with resignation.

Kortschenko stumbled to his feet as five crows fluttered away, while three remained on the table, jabbing viciously at the meat. He slammed his right hand against the wood—and was shocked by both the pain that surged up his arm and the feebleness of the sound he produced—and they disappeared through the roof. He staggered toward the door. The white light blinded him and, after covering his eyes with his sleeve, Kortschenko went straight for a snowdrift and fell to his knees. He buried his face in the snow, shoveling it into his mouth with his good hand and spitting out gobs of brown phlegm. After ten minutes, his mouth felt clean and his tongue regained its texture. He rose to his feet and, as he stretched, raising his arms as high as he could above his head, the numbing pain in his empty stomach returned. He took another handful of sweet-tasting snow and shoved it into his parched mouth.

Kortschenko raised his wet face to the unsparing sky. He had returned to the realm of the living and, as the wind cooled his battered cheeks, he felt an inexplicable sense of gratitude for the serenity around him. How peaceful and comfortable his life had been: *wie ruhig und gemütlich*. Would it ever return to that wonderful condition, in which everything had its rightful place and memories served not as a reminder of his awful present but as a sturdy bridge between the past and the future?

He recalled sledding outside Vienna on the Bisamberg— the impatient climb and the rapid descent through the sprays of snow and ice, followed by a thinly cut and crisp Wiener Schnitzel, a cucumber salad with just enough chopped parsley, and a sweet Kracherl at his parents' favorite Heuriger, where Fräulein Annerl always gave him a large pretzel and his father had too much to drink and then reminisced about the war, about the Bolsheviks who were cowards, about the glorious charge across the endless steppes, about the tragically brief capture of Kyiv, about the remarkable generosity of the peasants, about the gut-wrenching retreat through the thick mud. Where was Fräulein Annerl now and would she recognize him in the haggard wreck that he had become? Almost reluctantly, Kortschenko stepped back inside.

"We should explore the other huts," he mumbled. "Perhaps we'll find something."

"Another mouse?" Pieracki said irritably. He was sitting near the table, adjusting the splint on his bad knee and spitting every few seconds.

"The cannibals are somewhere in this village." Von Mecklenburg was reclining at the base of the oven. "Do not forget that, gentlemen. *Und dann die Polizei.* They may arrive any day now."

"That would almost be a relief." Kortschenko ran his hands through his hair. "A jail cell cannot possibly be any worse than this."

Von Mecklenburg affected a smile.

"But Siberia can, *mein lieber Freund*. Believe me when I tell you that none of us would survive long. We would stand in our excrement in the cattle cars and we would die and they would dump us along the tracks with hundreds of others. And we would lie there until the wolves came and tore our dead bodies to pieces. A cheerful prospect, *nicht wahr*?" Von Mecklenburg struggled to his feet and stood against the oven with his arms crossed.

"I have a better suggestion, *meine Herren*. Let us have a cigarette before we go—*bitte*. Herr Golub and I smoked one last night. I confess that it was quite good, actually." He looked at the ground thoughtfully.

"You know, this is where he sat when he died."

"It's almost as if he knew he was a condemned man, isn't it?" Pieracki said.

"He enjoyed it immensely. I think he had a premonition."

"Killing the dead woman," Kortschenko interjected. "That's what broke him. How could he live after that? How could he *want* to live after that? He lost his will to live after that. Did you notice that? He lost his will to live after that. And how could he live after that?"

*

The cigarette alleviated their hunger and sharpened their sense of alertness and the men left the hut in a more optimistic frame of mind. The dappled sky was grayish white, with bits of ultramarine blue shining through and creating ripples of light on the surface of the dull white snow. A row of crows fidgeted on the upper branches of the twisted apple trees opposite their hut. Except for an occasional caw, there was complete stillness. As the men listened to the unnatural calm, their optimism metamorphosed into a sense of dread and impending doom. Existential *Angst* could be fatal and von Mecklenburg knew that the *Endzeitstimmung* had to be dispelled before it demoralized them and destroyed their instinct for survival.

"My estate," he said, "is often as quiet as this. And the land is just as even. Do you believe me, gentlemen, when I say that I can imagine no more beautiful land in the world?"

"Are your holdings in Prussia, Herr Graf?" Kortschenko

asked, grateful for the distraction.

"East Prussia. The von Mecklenburgs are one of the oldest families in Germany."

"And," Pieracki said, hoping to sustain the change of mood, "one of the grandest."

But the count's smile faded as soon as Pieracki had finished speaking. The grandest of families had been shattered by the vagaries of an ill-tempered *fortuna* that had left his wife and children dead and him with nothing. As he contemplated his sad fate, he spoke with an unconcealed grief that verged on the dread he so desperately wanted to circumvent.

"Alas, *meine Herren*, the von Mecklenburgs are *kaputt*—like Deutschland. The war destroyed everything: our house, our crops, our barns, our lands, our animals. The front passed through it two, maybe three, times."

Just who was speaking? Kortschenko heard the German's voice, but it was the unfortunate Kateryna Fedorivna's sad words that resounded in his mind. How ironic for a nobleman and a peasant to have shared the same fate! And how tragic that he should have to bear witness to both! And yet, how fitting for such a role to have fallen upon a poet. After all, who but a poet could appreciate the full depth of the tragedy that had befallen them?

"How sad," he said, "but"—he spoke with forced enthusiasm—"at least you are alive!"

Von Mecklenburg appeared not to hear.

"I was away and there was no one to tend to matters. And then, after the soldiers, the fighting, and the refugees swept through like locusts, there was nothing and no one left and nothing to do anymore."

"A tragedy, Herr Graf, a tragedy," Kortschenko mumbled.

"*Alles war kaputt*—except for the house in Wannsee. And so I decided to serve my Fatherland at its time of greatest need."

"And you serve, even now, with Herr Hitler as your Chancellor. Only a man of great character and moral strength would—"

"Chancellors and presidents come and go, Herr Kortschenko, while we diplomats stay. It is our sacred duty—*unsere heilige Pflicht*—to serve the state, not its leaders."

"Well said, *mon ami*, well said, indeed!" Pieracki clapped his frozen hands. "Unfortunately, in your country as in mine, the leaders think they can run the state without us, but—"

"—they are mistaken?"

Von Mecklenburg smiled wanly as he finished Pieracki's thought. Alas, the sad reality was just the opposite: diplomats were irrelevant and leaders did whatever they liked. But what alternative was there to persisting? Who would tell the politicians "I told you so"? Who would instruct their successors on the finer points of statecraft? Especially after catastrophe struck—or struck *again*— and the wearisome process of building and rebuilding on the ruins of their errors had to be pursued by those who had served the Fatherland selflessly and honestly and quietly.

"Enough about politics, *meine Herren*. It is time for us to go."

*

It took almost half an hour for the men to climb across the snowdrifts between their hut and the next one. There, too, the windows and door were missing, but the thatched roof was also gone and only the rafters remained. They peered inside. The hut was full of snow. The splayed legs of three overturned benches disrupted the gently curved, smooth white surface. Only the space beneath the table was free of snow and there they found two corpses entangled in a macabre embrace. They appeared to be a mother and her child, but whether it was a boy or a girl was impossible to say from the skeletal frame bespattered with rotting flesh and dirty rags. A large crack ran down the middle of the oven and the door to the stove was half-open. The walls looked as if they had sustained a terrific shelling and no icons, embroideries, or farm implements adorned what remained of them.

Another hut stood no more than five meters away, but the men needed more than ten minutes to reach it. Its roof was intact and the shutterless windows resembled abandoned caves. The house consisted of two rooms. The first was bare, except for some benches and a twisted sickle hanging on a rusty nail. Von Mecklenburg took the implement and turned it over in his hands. He then led the way into the darkness of the second room. A powerful stench greeted the men as they stepped inside. They pressed their hands to their noses and mouths and needed a minute before they could see.

"Look," Pieracki coughed, "there are five—no, *six*—

bodies in here."

The corpses were all in various stages of decay. The ivory-colored eye sockets and nasal cavities stood out against the ebony skin drawn tightly across the skulls. Brownish bones protruded from the tips of fingers. Their chests were sunken and their legs extended in all directions, almost as if they had been detached from the torsos of broken dolls and dumped carelessly on a playground. An ankle or shin, sometimes all bone, sometimes draped with corrugated skin, would occasionally be visible. Three corpses were huddled together. The others lay in corners of the room. Two or possibly three rats scurried out of the room, past the men's unsteady legs.

"There is nothing here," von Mecklenburg pronounced. "*Nichts.*" His eyes burned from the stench and he sneezed repeatedly.

"The poor devils."

The next few huts resembled the one they had just left behind. One contained three dead bodies, another only two, still another three distinct piles—had they been fighting over scraps of food or had they been huddling for warmth?—with rotting, broken corpses in each. The smell was uniformly strong and, by the second or third hut, von Mecklenburg waited outside while the others explored the rooms. Pieracki found a long staff that could serve him as a crutch. Kortschenko extracted a crooked nail from one of the walls and cradled it in his good hand.

The next house was a complete ruin. Its roof was missing and two of the walls had caved in. They saw no bodies, probably because the hut had become uninhabitable many months ago. There appeared to be a small pile of blackened bones on the oven, but they couldn't see whether they were of human or animal origin. Nor did they care. Instead, their attention settled on a book, its pages fluttering in the wind, which lay on the ground near the entrance.

Kortschenko picked up the volume and examined it desultorily.

"It's a collection of Stalin's speeches." He hurled the book at the pile of bones and watched them scatter.

"They must have been communists—probably deported during the first collectivization campaign."

"We could use it to light a fire."

"*Nein*, Herr Graf, not Stalin. I would gladly burn him at the stake, but I refuse to warm my hands on his ashes."

They struggled through the snow for another fifteen minutes. This time, the shutters were still in place, as was the roof, although the door had been ripped off its hinges. Inside they found two rooms: an antechamber, where snow had piled up to under half a meter, and the main room, miraculously bereft of snow, where the oven, a long wooden table, two overturned benches, and three makeshift trunk-cots stood. They found four skeletons atop the oven and one on a trunk. The stench was ordinary, certainly no worse than the smell of their decaying bodies. A rat ran diagonally across the floor and disappeared into a hole in the wall. It was clear that this was where they would spend the night. Pieracki grabbed one of the benches, took a deep breath and set it upright, and sat down with a protracted groan.

"Should we get rid of the bodies?" Kortschenko asked.

"*Warum?*" von Mecklenburg said indifferently.

"Perhaps that one?" Kortschenko pointed at the corpse on the trunk. "Then each of us will have a place to sleep."

The count shook his head. "Why? They are not disturbing us and we are not disturbing them."

*

Kortschenko and von Mecklenburg stepped outside and immersed their sweaty faces in the snow. The sun had already set and the snow shimmered like a mountain lake. The trees and huts resembled ashen cut-outs against the coal sky. Soon everything would be impenetrably dark. A large bird, possibly an owl, glided gracefully over their heads. When their faces revived, the two men began gnawing at the delicious snow. *Wir sind ja Ratten*, von Mecklenburg thought. We are rats. Before, we ate rats. Now, we have become rats. Who, he wondered, would catch, skin, and eat them?

When they returned to the house, the German crawled onto the table, while the Ukrainian dropped down on a trunk next to the Pole. The slog through the snow had sapped them of their remaining strength. They lay quietly, but their hearts and minds were racing too fast for them to fall asleep.

"Who has the tobacco?" von Mecklenburg inquired.

Kortschenko grunted and brought the tin to the table. The

count took the box of matches from his pocket and examined the contents.

"We have two matches, *meine Herren*. I propose we smoke all the tobacco today. As to tomorrow, well, *morgen ist ein anderer Tag*—and we shall see what tomorrow holds in store for us. *D'accord?*"

When he and Kortschenko were done rolling three crooked cigarettes, the count took a match and struck it sharply against the side of the box. A bluish flash appeared and von Mecklenburg held the flame to the tip of the cigarette dangling from Kortschenko's mouth. The paper and tobacco sparkled and Kortschenko inhaled, producing a dark orange glow. Von Mecklenburg lit another cigarette and gave it to the Pole, who said "*merci*" and seized it greedily. The match sputtered and the flame went out, but von Mecklenburg held his cigarette to the glowing end of Kortschenko's and inhaled with a look of deep satisfaction on his face.

"*Komisch*, is it not? In Berlin, I can buy any brand of cigarettes I want, but no tobacco has ever tasted quite as good as this."

"Gauloises," Kortschenko announced. "Gauloises are my brand."

"*Wirklich?* I prefer Turkish, although I confess to finding American tobacco surprisingly good. I first smoked it in the war, when we came across some in the trenches." Von Mecklenburg smacked his lips.

"*Und dazu ein Gläschen Wein!*"

"A liter of Grüner Veltliner!" Kortschenko exclaimed. "In Grinzing. *Nein*—better still—in the Urbanikeller. Do you know the Urbani, Herr Graf? My father loved it. Oh, how he loved it! They would meet there every Friday—he and his Ukrainian émigré friends—and plot their revenge against the Bolsheviks over liters of wine and blood sausage with horseradish and thick slices of black bread."

"Yes, quite," the count replied, "the Urbani is excellent, but I confess to having a weakness for the Esterhazy, especially for the lower level, where the alcoholics congregate like Christians in the catacombs." Von Mecklenburg exhaled deeply, releasing a series of barely visible smoke rings.

"Ach, the smoke-filled back rooms! The loud talk and belly

laughs! The *Liptauerbrote!*"

The men fell silent. They pulled on their cigarettes and watched them grow smaller. Except for the three glowing ends, the room was pitch-black. Outside, the wind began blowing with a ferocity that rudely reminded them of where they really were.

"What do you think, *meine Herren?* Will we ever see our homes again?" von Mecklenburg asked. Before the others could answer, he continued:

"This accursed land. I have a sickle, but I cannot use it. We are in the breadbasket of Europe, but we have nothing to eat. How can that be? *Wie ist so etwas möglich?* Back in 1918, we lost the war and the retreat was humiliating, but at least we *could* retreat. Now— *nichts*, nothing at all. Neither forward, nor backward. All we can do is stay here. Amid this accursed whiteness!" Von Mecklenburg shook his head and closed his eyes.

"African savages fear the dark because they believe all manner of terrible creatures inhabit its invisible recesses. But this whiteness is much worse, *meine Herren.* It is infinitely worse. Nothing, not even the monstrous creatures of a primitive imagination, can live in its emptiness. I ask you, *meine Herren*: What can be worse than nothing?" The count answered his own question.

"Nothing. *Nichts ist schlimmer als nichts, meine Herren.* I can assure you that even the hell of the trenches and the appalling emptiness of *Niemandsland* were preferable to this—this white *nichts.*" Von Mecklenburg tossed the cigarette butt across the room.

"If there is a hell, *meine Herren,* then it is a perpetual famine in a perpetual winter."

Pieracki took a long drag on his cigarette and blew out a column of invisible smoke.

"*Mes amis*"—he had lifted himself up on his elbows—"we need a plan. We cannot just sit here and bemoan our fate. Or else this room will soon have three more corpses."

"What do you propose?" Kortschenko asked gloomily. "We have no strength. We have no food. We are trapped in a village surrounded by meter-high snow. And we have no idea where we are. I'm afraid the situation is hopeless."

"But not," von Mecklenburg chortled, "serious. Is that not what you Viennese say?"

"Only when we are sitting in a wine garden, Herr Graf,

watching the sun set, drinking our Veltliner, and pondering the meaning of life." Kortschenko couldn't refrain from smiling. "No question stays unanswered for long in a Heuriger!"

The Ukrainian's cigarette had gone out and he crushed the remnants with his fingers. He raised them to his nose and sniffed. They should have reeked of tobacco, but instead he smelled only excrement.

"The comrade would have said that communism has all the answers," Pieracki noted. "He was wrong, of course, but at least he believed in some—"

Von Mecklenburg exploded: "Comrade Golub is directly responsible for this devastation! We are here—and make no mistake, *meine Herren*, we are *dying* here—because of what he was, what he did, and what he stood for."

"Of course, he was a Jew."

"He was a *communist*," stated von Mecklenburg with a vehemence that surprised him, "and that is infinitely worse! *That* is unforgivable. The world is better off without the likes of Comrade Golub. Just take a look at these damned peasants! There were hundreds, maybe thousands, in that graveyard. And every house has more corpses.

"It never ends, *meine Herren*, it *never* ends! The numbers grow and grow and the death refuses to go away. *Der Tod ist überall.*"

Both saddened and shocked by his weakness, the count realized that he had succumbed to the irresistible pessimism he had vowed to fight, but there was no going back.

"If these wretched Ukrainians could not save themselves, how can we?"

For several seconds no one spoke. To disagree with von Mecklenburg was impossible. But to agree was tantamount to suicide. Kortschenko resumed smelling his fingers, while Pieracki sighed.

"We are in *Zugzwang, mes amis.* Since there is nothing to be said and nothing to be done," he said, "I suggest we go to sleep. And tomorrow—well, tomorrow is a new day, perhaps a new start." He took one final drag on the cigarette and watched the remains burn out in his fingers.

"I also have a suggestion. We should sleep as close together as possible—to stay warm. And for safety. Drag the table and trunk closer to me, please. I would, but I cannot." Pieracki tried bending his knee, but abandoned the effort due to the intense pain.

"I'm afraid my knee is useless. There will be no walking for me tomorrow."

"*If*," von Mecklenburg grunted, "there is a tomorrow."

The men lay silently, in the all-encompassing darkness, listening to the wind howl and their hearts beat, until they fell asleep. Their tired bodies were quite still, almost like corpses, so that even the secret police, had they chanced upon them, might have thought they were stone cold dead. And indeed, their breathing was barely perceptible and, if a mirror had been placed to their nostrils, it would have taken an expert eye to see the moisture. Outside, the diaphanous cloud cover failed to conceal a luminous golden sliver that hung like a finely sharpened scimitar in the dark night sky. Inside, two rats emerged from their hole and crossed the room to the oven and the corpses. The men heard nothing, sleeping soundly, sometimes twitching or quietly moaning—for no obvious reason.

*

Kortschenko lowered his feet to the ground and, careful not to bump into the table or bench where the others lay snoring, made his way uncertainly to the door. The hut was icy and it took him a while to realize, through the haze of his half-conscious state, that the clattering sound he heard was produced by his own teeth. There was no wind, giant snowflakes fell lazily to the ground, and, thanks to the barely visible moon, the snowdrifts and trees had acquired a lush and variegated tonality that he would have called, in almost any other circumstances, extraordinarily beautiful: *ausserordentlich wunderschön*. Kortschenko vaguely remembered such landscapes from family trips to his father's relatives in some nameless village outside Lemberg. His Austrian mother sniffed at the unwashed peasants and their crude ways, but his father shrugged and insisted that he had finally come home, that he loved the smell of the cow pastures and the coldness of the water in the well, and that he would never leave—until, of course, they did leave, much to the boy's disappointment and his mother's relief at being able to take strolls with her lace-lined Paisley parasol along the Ring or the Graben once again.

Oddly, he had to relieve himself more often now, even though he drank almost nothing. His skin felt drier, tougher, less resilient—scabrous. Was his body shriveling like a raisin? Was it giving up the ghost? He buttoned his pants and breathed in the crisp night air. His teeth had calmed themselves and he tried to listen to the impenetrable silence. He dipped his good hand into the snow, felt it melt, and lapped up the water. His bearded face felt foreign against his palm. He cupped his hand over his mouth and exhaled. His breath stank: small wonder, after a diet of snow, squirrel, and mouse.

Why in God's name was he here? He should have known that this was no place for a poet, especially one accustomed to the fine cakes, delicious coffees, and good wines Vienna had to offer in such glorious abundance. The second floor of the Café Central and not Kharkiv was where he should have pursued revolution and national liberation. Wasn't the pen mightier than the sword? Besides, bad poetry could also serve the cause—but not here, not where books were banned, readers languished in piles of corpses, and the language was being systematically destroyed.

A muffled crackling wafted toward him from somewhere to his right. Kortschenko stepped back against the wall and, holding his breath while his heart raced, listened attentively. There it was again, so faint as to be almost inaudible. When he strained his ears and closed his eyes, an unmistakable crunching, like the sound of heavy boots on gravel, could be heard. Were the boots approaching or receding? He couldn't tell. He closed his eyes again. Now the sound appeared to be coming from his left. Was that an echo or the wind or were there footsteps all around? Kortschenko crouched down and place his ear to a patch of bare ground. There was no doubt about it. Someone was walking in the snow, close enough to the hut to be within earshot.

Kortschenko squatted behind a blue snowdrift and squinted into the darkness. The crunching appeared to come from his right again. He focused his eyes and thought he saw shadowy figures moving slowly in the distance. Or were they just the shadows that the moon cast upon the snow banks? He rubbed his eyes and focused again. No, this time he was certain: the shadows were human shapes and there appeared to be at least three. Were they villagers? That was possible, but, considering that they had only seen dead bodies in the huts, unlikely. The cannibals? All too likely. The secret police? At this time of night? But, then again, *warum nicht?* After all, the GPU *chekists* were masters of the midnight knock and a nighttime surprise attack would be perfectly consistent with their modus operandi.

Kortschenko held his breath as he crawled back into the hut. Von Mecklenburg was awake and seized him gruffly by the arm. Kortschenko placed a finger to his lips and nudged Pieracki, who awoke with a start. The Ukrainian breathed "Be quiet" into his ear and crouched down between the two.

"We have guests."

"Who?"

"I don't know, but I heard footsteps and saw shadows."

"Are you certain?"

"Yes—I think so."

"How many?"

"Three, maybe four—maybe more. It's hard to see."

"Are you sure—absolutely?"

"Yes. I think so. It's dark outside. Still..."

"Very well, we must assume you saw them." Von Mecklenburg dropped his feet to the floor and turned to Pieracki.

"How is your knee? Can you get up?"

"I think so." Pieracki placed his good leg on the floor and followed with his bad leg. "It's very stiff. I can barely move it."

"That is good," von Mecklenburg said. "It would be worse if you were in pain. Rub it, gently, and bend your knee—slowly. It will loosen up quickly."

"What should we do?" Kortschenko realized that he was shaking.

"Nothing," the count replied. "The two of you stay here, in the corner—over there. I will take a look outside."

Es war jetzt oder nie, von Mecklenburg thought, as he bent over and dashed to the doorway, almost as if he were running along a narrow trench just before the shelling began and all hell broke loose. He could feel the adrenalin coursing through his arteries and veins. He fell to his hands and knees and crawled outside, positioning himself behind a sloping snowdrift. He could see the shadows and hear a gravelly sound and male voices coming from somewhere on the right. The wind had resumed and it carried them in his direction. They were speaking, calmly—did that exclude the possibility of the cannibals?—but indistinctly. Von

Mecklenburg dropped to his belly and—as so often during the war, when he had led patrols across No Man's Land to spy on the enemy and return with prisoners—began crawling, as quietly as a python in the Amazonian rain forest. The snow was easier to negotiate than the upturned earth and thick mud of war-time. There were no snipers, no craters, no flares, no machine-gun fire, no unexploded shells, no barbed wire, no mines, no bombs, no limbs, no corpses. It was just a matter of burrowing through the white snow and hoping that *fortuna* was on his side. He had done it many times before, most recently in this very country, back in late 1918. And if he could do it then, he could do it now, again. It was all a question of timing: *Es war jetzt oder nie.* He crawled along the path leading up to the house, paused briefly, peered just above the flat-top surface of the snow, and fell back to the ground. There were no snipers. The enemy sat in his trenches far away. The coast was clear. The snow to his right was one meter high. He took a deep breath, dove into it, and disappeared. *Es war jetzt oder nie.*

*

It took twenty minutes and much maneuvering and silent cursing, but Kortschenko and Pieracki finally succeeded in pushing the table into a corner, just to the left of the doorway, and scrambled under it. Someone looking in wouldn't see them, especially if they held their bodies pressed into the corner. Pieracki leaned back against the wall and exercised his knee, while Kortschenko sat cross-legged and, resting his broken hand on his thigh, massaged it with the fingers of his right hand.

"My brother and I would hide under the kitchen table when we were boys," Pieracki said with a chuckle. "It was just like this. And he would sit just like you, like an Indian. We had a large kitchen and the cook—good God! I just remembered she was a rotund Ukrainian woman from Równo—would hand us the bowls in which she'd prepared fillings for cakes. We raced to see who could lick the bowl clean. I was Old Chatterhand and he was Winnetou." Pieracki grinned.

"Old Chatterhand usually won."

Kortschenko was in no mood for the Pole's chatter.

"*Hören Sie bitte auf.*" He spoke as steadily as his rattled nerves permitted. "Please stop. We are in great danger and, in case you hadn't noticed, our present circumstances are terribly humiliating." His ears were pounding, a horrible death might be lurking just a few meters away, they were completely helpless and utterly defenseless, and he had heard more than enough about the past from the German.

"May I also remind you that this is not a Karl May story," he said sternly, "that the cannibals are not Indians, and that we are not children."

"Of course we're not, *mon ami*, of course we're not, but what else are we to do? When the old man returns, we'll plan—"

"What?"

Pieracki shrugged. "Perhaps an escape, perhaps resistance. Perhaps nothing."

"With your knee and my hand? *Nein*," Kortschenko shook his head, "I fear we will stay here, under this table, until they come for us."

"Well, our sisters never found us."

"Obviously. They weren't looking."

It was best to ignore the poet's ill humor. Pieracki ran his fingers along the contours of his face. He was struck by how pointed his features had become. His cheeks were sunken, his nose felt large, his double chin was gone, and his complexion was probably as ashen as that of the others. He suspected he wouldn't recognize himself in a mirror. Would the girls? Perhaps. Would his mother? Probably. How could mothers forget their beloved sons? He tried to conjure up an image of her face, but failed.

"When did you last eat?" Pieracki asked.

"I'm not sure: one or two days before they threw me in that van. And you?"

"At the consulate. It must be at least a week ago." Pieracki scratched his head and realized that his greasy hair probably smelled as badly as he did.

"All I think of is food, but I no longer remember when I had my last meal." He giggled like a school boy.

"But I do remember what we ate: cabbage and pork with boiled potatoes and pickled mushrooms. And we drank *wódka*. *Matko Boska*, did we ever drink *wódka*! Let me tell you something, *mon ami*. Our consulate knows how to organize an elegant reception. Why do you think I was wearing tails?"

"Is that when they arrested you?"

"Right after, as I was walking home. I needed the air and

the night wasn't too cold. I hadn't walked more than a hundred meters when a black van pulled up alongside me and three gorillas in leather jackets sprang out and pushed me inside. They knocked me on the head and, when I awoke, my hands had been tied and my eyes were covered with a hood. Then they dumped me in that cell."

"Yes, I see. And how long did they transport you?"

"About five hours after I regained consciousness, but it could've been a day until then. Or more. And you?"

"I was on a train to Kharkiv, asleep, and the guards stormed in at one of the stations and dragged me off." Kortschenko appeared to be deliberating.

"The rest is no different from your story. Well, except that I am a poet."

"Indeed, *ein Dichter aus Wien!* Forgive me for asking, *mon ami,* but are you a good poet?"

"Good? *Eine gute Frage!*" Kortschenko snorted. "A good question! Am I Goethe? Am I Mickiewicz? Am I Shevchenko?" The questions were obviously rhetorical and the Ukrainian quickly changed the topic.

"And they never told you why? They never told you what they were charging you with?"

"*Nie.*"

"As with me."

"But you're a Ukrainian nationalist, *mon ami!* It's no mystery why they arrested you."

"Yes, it's true: I belong to a political movement." Kortschenko lowered his voice as if in confidence. "Our goal is the destruction of Russian communism and the liberation of Ukraine."

"So you were here," Pieracki said deliberately, "on an important mission? A poet on a clandestine political mission? Pardon my saying so, *mon ami,* but that is highly unusual. Don't you agree?"

"We are building a network in Soviet Ukraine. My assignment was to contact our people and form a cell."

"You were betrayed," Pieracki said matter-of-factly. "Your people sent a poet and the Bolsheviks were waiting with open arms. It was almost too easy for them, I wager. No underground organization sends an inexperienced—you forgive me for saying so?—writer on such an important and dangerous mission. Unless, that is, the organization is penetrated, as yours must be." He ended with a ring of finality.

"You can be quite certain of that."

Kortschenko frowned. "How do you know?"

"I know," Pieracki shrugged. "Pan Kortschenko, even the Polish security service has agents in your organization. Why shouldn't the Bolsheviks? They have many more resources and much more skill. They are ruthless. They are adults. We are children in comparison to them. We hide under tables. They organize mass famines."

"*We?* You mean *you?*"

Pieracki's tone became distinctly formal. "It is my honor and privilege to defend the Polish state, Pan Kortschenko. You must know that I would die for Poland. All Polish patriots would. You must know that, too."

"So the Polish minister of interior, Bronisław Pieracki, is—?"

"A relative—a distant relative, but a relative."

"Then we are enemies, Herr Pieracki."

"Out there, perhaps." Pieracki waved his hand in some uncertain direction. "But here, under this table, we are just little boys. *If* we survive, Pan Kortschenko, *if* we survive and return to our homes, *then* we will have ample time and opportunity to kill each other"—Pieracki snickered—"as befits true enemies. In the meantime, the barricades are very far away. We are hiding from cannibals under a peasant table. My knee hurts and your hand is swollen. I think we can put our knives away."

The Pole had seen through him. Moreover, despite his genteel appearance, despite his foppishness, despite his evident love of the good life, Pieracki was a professional—and, much to his chagrin and shame, he had underestimated the Pole completely. Then again, he was a poet, not a professional; and, besides, the Pole had a point. It was absurd to settle scores while crouching under a table. The two fell silent for a minute until, finally, Kortschenko spoke.

"And where is home?"

"Lwów."

"I was born just outside *Lviv.*" Kortschenko was careful to emphasize the Ukrainian name.

"A beautiful city, *mon ami*, and a wonderful opera! And the restaurants and cafés and dancing halls! And, of course, the women! Can you guess where we lived?"

"It will be ours someday."

"Oh, how serious of you, Pan Kortschenko! I talk to you of the beauty of our native city and you want to fight over cobblestones again. That is the problem with you nationalists, *mon ami*. So serious—you must learn to enjoy life."

*

Kortschenko fell silent again. The Pole was smart, always managing to portray himself as the voice of reason and him, the poet, as a brute. He recalled the discussions he witnessed among the Ukrainian émigrés in the Café Central. They calculated the strategic consequences of every new development, from the rise of Mussolini to the collapse on Wall Street to the triumphs of the Nazis to the purges in the Soviet Union. They would have known what to say in his place and Kortschenko regretted that he had always been more interested in the fiery women and their excited bosoms than in the arguments they were making. The Pole was obviously right about the presence of spies in their midst. How could such a boisterous group of patriots not be penetrated by enemy agents, especially in so open a setting, where everyone with an opinion or the money to buy a round of drinks was always welcome?

"May I suggest you worry about the new Germany, Herr Pieracki? Have you read what the National Socialists have to say about *Lebensraum*? That is *you*, Herr Pieracki. *Lebensraum* means Poland."

"If we fall, then so will your beloved Ukraine."

"Not if Germany supports us."

"The Nazis hate all Slavs."

"But they hate Jews and communism even more."

"True," Pieracki nodded thoughtfully, "that is quite true. But it is small consolation for you, or for us, if they destroy us all. No, *mon ami*, the matter is both much more simple and much more complex than—"

Kortschenko held up his hand. "Quiet!" he hissed. "Did you hear something? I think I just heard something."

"*Co?*"

"Voices."

"The same voices?"

"I don't know. Where *is* that absurd German?"

"He's probably outside, reliving his days in the trenches. Did you notice, *mon ami?* The old man lives in the past, in the last century. He doesn't understand the present and is quite incapable of anticipating the future. He is decent, as far as Germans go, but useless."

"If they catch him, they catch us."

"Or not," Pieracki countered. "If they catch him, we could be saved."

"Only if they eat him."

"*Exactement.*"

As the two men strained to hear, they fell asleep. Just before he drifted into unconsciousness, Pieracki remembered something odd. Whenever he and his brother hid under the table, his mother had always announced that the cookies and cakes and iced tea she prepared were for guests who, he now realized, never materialized.

*

They awoke in a few minutes, perhaps fifteen, certainly no more than thirty. The wind whistled through the windows and swept past the doorway. It was impossible to hear anything anymore, either footsteps or voices. Pieracki groaned. His knee still hurt; his shoulder had also begun to ache, perhaps from leaning against the cold wall. As he tried to shift his weight, his head struck the table and a feeble knock reverberated throughout the house. Kortschenko started, seizing Pieracki's arm tightly with his right hand. They remained frozen for an instant until Kortschenko released his grip and sat back.

"Did the German take the sickle?"

"No, it's on the table. And the staff is near my cot."

"We should have them on hand," Kortschenko said. "Just in case."

"They won't do much good against guns, *mon ami.*"

"But at least one of them will join us in hell."

"Really, *mon ami?* Have you ever killed a man?"

"Of course not."

"Neither have I. They tell me it's much harder than one

imagines it to be, especially if it's just you and him, *tête-à-tête*, so to speak. I think that's the problem, *mon ami*—the eyes. How can you kill someone who is looking you in your eyes?"

"If it's kill or be killed, what choice does one have?"

"You Ukrainians," Pieracki sighed. "You're much too serious and—"

"There are times when one must face death boldly and unflinchingly, like a man."

"—you're much too willing to die. Alas, we Poles are the same. We think there is glory in being senselessly slaughtered on a muddy field of battle by a superior foe. But the trick, *mon ami*, is to live for your nation, isn't it? The trick is to outwit that foe and make him pay for his mistakes with his life. Anybody can commit suicide, even a nationalist."

"And you—you are not a nationalist?"

"Of course, but spies are clever. We let others do the dying. I'm surprised you don't do the same. After all, what are you if not a spy?"

Kortschenko felt the blood rush to his face. Did the Pole notice? Probably—after all, he seemed to notice everything.

"You boarded a train in Vienna. Your assignment was to organize a clandestine cell somewhere in Ukraine. You succeeded. And you betrayed nothing to your captors." Pieracki paused for a pregnant second.

"Or did you?"

"They never asked me to," Kortschenko stammered. Did the Pole notice the hesitation in his voice? He knew his answer was unconvincing. How could a spy believe that his interrogators had failed to press him for vital secrets? Obviously, Pieracki could not. No one could. Indeed, neither could he.

"Exactly!" Pieracki cried with excessive enthusiasm. "You and I, *mon ami*—we like to think we would never betray the cause, that we would withstand all manner of tortures, never breathe a single indiscreet word. But what joy we feel, what inexpressible joy that they never asked, never applied their tongs or beat us with sticks or prodded us like cattle! Isn't that right, Pan Kortschenko?" The Pole, clearly, had seen through all his evasions.

"Who are the real heroes? You and I or these miserable peasants who chose starvation over joining a collective farm? I can tell you right now: I would have joined on the spot. Death is not worth a piece of land."

"You are not a peasant," Kortschenko said feebly, "that's why. If you were, if you believed your whole life was bound up with this black earth, you'd speak differently."

"I suspect you're right, Pan Kortschenko. It's true, *oczywiście.* I am an urban man and I do not understand this mystical attraction of the soil. I adore the opera, cafés, and restaurants. I like sidewalks and cobblestone streets and smokestacks and the roar of motors and machines. To me, soil is just dirt, nothing more, and the peasants are, as the good Marx once put it, just a sack of potatoes."

"But *I* understand the Ukrainian village, Herr Pieracki. *You* are a foreigner here. *I* am the prodigal son."

"Who, then, is your father?" Pieracki tittered. "Who will embrace you and welcome you home? Comrade Stalin?"

Once again, the Pole had scored a point and he, the wordsmith, was at a loss for words.

"The people—the people are with us."

"The people?"

This was the second time in recent days that the people had been invoked and Pieracki decided that he could no longer keep his irony from spilling over into sarcasm.

"The *people*? *What* people? The corpses on that oven? The corpses in that mound? There is no *narod, mon ami,* except in your imagination. I have traveled throughout this country. The people— *your* people—are all in graves or jails or cattle cars. If you want to overthrow Soviet power, Pan Kortschenko, I'm afraid you will have to do it on your own. No one will help you. Not even the skeletons.

"They cannot," he spoke with genuine sadness in his voice, "even help themselves, these people of yours. The communists take away their food and they do nothing. They take away their land and they do nothing. They take away their lives and they die miserably on trunks and ovens and in graveyards."

"But there *were*—there *are*—rebellions," Kortschenko protested, "even armed rebellions. We have information, reports: the peasants resisted, there was bloodshed. The indomitable Ukrainian peasantry has always fought back, since the time of Khmelnytsky, when, as you well know—"

"And what difference did they make?" Could the

Ukrainian poet really do no better than invoke the anti-Polish Cossack uprisings of the 1640s?

"No, *mon ami*, this Soviet monster is too strong. You need help, *our* help. Your Petliura was right, you know. He and Piłsudski almost changed the course of history in 1920."

"They failed."

"But they almost succeeded!"

"And Petliura betrayed Galicia."

"A small province! But he almost won Ukraine. That's why the Marshall was able to restore Polish statehood, *mon ami*. He was a strategist. He made compromises when necessary. He remained firm when necessary."

"And he betrayed Petliura, his ally, when necessary."

"He put him aside. He let him go, but only when it became clear that your Otaman had nothing to offer. That is the essence of good strategy, *mon ami*. Besides, why didn't your Petliura betray our Piłsudski? Why are you Ukrainians so—pardon my saying so, *mon ami*—principled? Only history's losers believe in principles. Winners manipulate them. Winners make them."

"And yet you say we need your help," Kortschenko said weakly.

"Poland may betray you, *mon ami*, but we will never destroy you. We cannot; we are too weak. Germany will betray you *and* destroy you. So will Russia. Your choice is unenviable, I know. But there is none other."

*

They fell silent and listened to the wind. Pieracki resumed rubbing his knee, while Kortschenko placed his broken hand on his stomach and watched it rise and fall. His body was wasting away, his bones were disintegrating, he reeked of death—and yet his stomach, absurdly, was growing. This was, he knew, a sign of starvation. The two of them were hovering between life and death. How could Piłsudski or Petliura save them? How could Hitler or Stalin? They couldn't. No one could.

"Where do you think the German is?" Kortschenko asked. "He should've been back by now."

"We heard no shots or shouts. If they had captured him, we would have heard something. He would have tried to warn us. And remember: he is a confused old man. I wouldn't be surprised if he got lost."

"Perhaps he's frozen?" Kortschenko wondered. "When he set out, the wind was calm. Perhaps he lost his way when it began snowing again? The poor man may be going in circles in the snow."

Pieracki couldn't resist smirking.

"The old man needs no snow to go in circles, *mon ami*. And besides, with my leg and your hand, what are we to do? No, *mon ami*, the old man will return or he will not return. Our place is not underground or in the trenches. It is beneath this table. Here is where we shall make our Thermopylae."

Thermopylae! Thermopylae, indeed! The image struck Kortschenko as so pathetic, so ridiculous, and so preposterous that he couldn't help but laugh out loud.

"But we are missing two hundred and ninety-eight Spartans!"

The two men began giggling uncontrollably, as much from the evident absurdness of their hopeless circumstances as from their resemblance to two small boys who had broken a vase and were hiding from their red-faced mother.

"But, but," Kortschenko gasped for breath, "Lviv is still ours!"

"In that case, we take Vienna!" Pieracki replied, equally out of breath. "No—better still!—we get the wine gardens of Grinzing!"

"*Nein, nein, nein!* That won't do! *Das geht überhaupt nicht!* You can have the Café Griensteidl. We keep the Central."

"Ah, so you are foisting those insufferable Viennese literati on my poor country. Very well, *mon ami*: in that case we also insist on the Sacher."

"As long as we keep the *Sachertorten!*"

"The Hofburg for you and Schönbrunn for us?"

"Excellent!" cried Kortschenko. "We take the Art History Museum and you take the Natural History Museum."

"Poland would prefer it the other way, but so be it. As compensation, we get Klimt and Kokoschka."

"Keep them. A Cossack nation needs only the Lipizzaners!"

The game had gone far enough and Pieracki fell silent.

"Look," he spoke rapidly and without hesitation, "my knee

should be better in a day or two, especially if I don't walk. Your hand will also improve. We must try to leave this hellhole. There must be other villages around here. Perhaps they're not as devastated. Perhaps we'll stumble upon a collective farm. The collective farmers are hungry, but they have food. We might find a good peasant. Perhaps get shelter and survive this winter. And then, when spring comes—"

"What then?"

"When spring comes, we walk west, *mon ami*. We walk to Poland and salvation."

*

Sleep came easily beneath the table and they slept for three or four hours, fitfully, like sentries listening to errant sounds and reacting to suspicious noises. Pieracki's hands would sometimes tighten and, when they did, his lips pursed, as if he were whistling or expressing surprise. Kortschenko would occasionally moan, but whether from a dream or a nightmare or from his pulsating hand was impossible to say. At one point, the Ukrainian's whole body shook convulsively; he snapped back his head and struck the wall and awoke. As he peered out from under the table, he saw two wavy lines framing the window and faintly illuminating the room. The air felt fetid.

Kortschenko slid along the walls, crossed the antechamber, and poked his head through the doorway. There was no wind and no snow. As usual, the sky was covered with a thick layer of moist cotton and the crows were sitting on the apple trees. Otherwise, he saw nothing and heard only their sporadic cries. He knew the birds were indifferent to his fate, but their caws struck him as impertinent cackles intended to mock him and his impotence.

He had seen the shadows and heard the voices somewhere to his right, but there was nothing there now, except for the snow-covered rooftops and, in the distance, the copper dome of a small church. If they could only manage to creep past the huts to the right, they should eventually come to a larger road leading to another village. And if he and the Pole could actually manage to leave in a day or two—which was to say *if* they could survive for that long—then that, clearly, was the thing to do.

There appeared to be a little gully in the snow. The old

soldier had probably crawled along that path, hoping to get a closer look at the shadows, to determine what they were saying and who they were. Had von Mecklenburg been captured by the cannibals? Or was the count lying dead, frozen, his face white, his lips blue, somewhere in the snow—like a corpse in his beloved No Man's Land? The German would not be coming back: Kortschenko felt it in his gut. There would be no more moralizing, no more lecturing, no more war stories. The absurd aristocrat must have known that he was embarking on a suicide mission and he was probably happy—perhaps even fulfilled—to have had the opportunity to engage in one last hurrah. After all, he had lost everything, including his country. He had said so himself. What did he have to live for? Why should he fear death? Indeed, wasn't he just like the sad Kateryna Fedorivna, the woman Golub had killed? Yes, the German was gone for good—and they were on their own, he had a broken hand, and the Pole could barely walk.

Kortschenko dipped his face into the snow. The coldness was refreshing and his face and eyes came alive. He ate the snow furiously, until his tongue and lips turned numb and his stomach felt sated. He and his father had eaten snow on the Bisamberg, while waiting their turn on the sledding queue. Papa had said it would keep him alert and he was right. But then, on the mountain top, the snow had been a treat, like a wonderful ice cream dessert. Here, amid the corpses, the snow was only a condition, a void, that heralded more of the same and promised nothing. A potent mixture of sadness, fear, and anxiety overcame Kortschenko and he sucked in his breath in the sudden realization that *he*—and not the old German—was trapped in No Man's Land. The Pole was right. He was a rank amateur. And the German was right. He was a boy—*ein kleiner Bub*. His place was the Ringstrasse on a warm summer evening, amid the stout ladies with their poodles and frilly bonnets.

Kortschenko plunged his hands into the snow and rubbed his face and neck until they hurt. The physical exertion both revived and exhausted him and he felt as if he were on a carousel that was threatening to spin out of control. He extended his hand against the wall and steadied himself. Once the kaleidoscope of colors before his eyes had vanished, he unbuttoned his trousers and watched the stream of pink-gold urine glisten and steam as it carved out zigzagging crevices in the snow. He buttoned his trousers, grabbed some snow, and made a small ball. When he crawled back under the table, Pieracki was already awake. The Pole had a wretched expression on his face, like that of a chronic insomniac who had spent another sleepless night pacing the floor. Kortschenko gave him the snowball. Instinctively, Pieracki bit into it, as if it were a freshly baked roll, and winced.

"It hurts." He consumed it greedily, nonetheless, and then rubbed his hands against his cheeks and eyes.

"*Dziękuję.*"

"The German is definitely gone. He won't be coming back."

"Dead?"

"I suppose so. The old soldier appears to have met his end in the snow."

"Did you see anyone?"

"No, there is nothing but snow."

"But the shadows, the voices—they must be somewhere."

"Perhaps they've gone. Or perhaps they're asleep. There is nothing—only snow—*nichts ausser diesem furchtbaren Schnee.* How is your leg?"

"It hurts, but less than before. And, *voila!*" Pieracki cradled his knee in his hands. "The swelling has gone down a bit."

"Will you be able to walk tomorrow? We shouldn't stay here much longer. Those shadows will be back."

"I think so."

"There must be a road leading from the village. If we keep going in that direction"—Kortschenko pointed to his right, without being sure that was correct—"we should come to a road. There has to be a road. Every village has one."

"And then we'll walk west."

"I hear the Zbruch River is narrow—easy to cross."

Pieracki nodded.

"Our sentries patrol the Polish side. They will protect us. And I know where we can cross. There are special areas our agents use when they come and go. Truth to tell, *mon ami*, I have been there myself."

*

As the Pole was speaking, Kortschenko's head sank and he was soon snoring. Pieracki took a deep breath and tried extending his left leg. His knee still hurt, but only when the leg was fully straightened. He raised his knee to his chin and massaged it. Then he lowered the knee and extended his leg—up and down, up and down—until, suddenly, his bladder felt very full. There was no need to go outside and risk slipping. The other side of the room would suffice.

Pieracki slid out from under the table. After placing both hands on the edge, he extended his right leg to the side, propped himself on his left leg, and raised the rest of his inert body. This simple maneuver left him gasping and his pulse racing. After standing still with both hands on his heaving chest, he began sliding along the wall, his left shoulder pressed against its rough surface, using it to keep his balance and to relieve the pressure on his knee. He made a turn, ever so gradually, past the oven and toward the corner positioned diagonally across from the table. As he stopped to catch his breath, he became aware of a pungent smell he hadn't noticed before. It had to be the skeletons on the oven. He held his nose and turned his eyes upward. He could see four skulls; they appeared to be glowing incandescently. Scraps of flesh, probably black and rotting, or the remnants of intestines were almost certainly hidden among the rags and accounted for the stench.

The sight of the neatly arrayed skulls filled him with an anger bordering on rage. The odor was distressing, but it was only an irritation of his olfactory senses. He could explain it and he could live with it. But how was he to explain and live with this passivity, this universal willingness to die like flies? It was beyond comprehension: the entire family, hungry and weak, climbed atop the oven and just lay down, waiting for extinction. Despite the Ukrainian's assurances to the contrary, there was no resistance, no struggle—*nothing*. These miserable people simply accepted their fates and welcomed their own annihilation. Would the Poles also opt for *nic*? Or would they fight? To the finish? To the last man, woman, and child? He wasn't so sure.

Pieracki resumed his journey and reached the corner. With his right leg extended and his weight placed on his left, he let his trousers drop to his knees. How absurd and pathetic, he thought, to be standing naked and vulnerable, with his genitals fully exposed, in a dark hut in the middle of the Ukrainian steppe. And such a man was supposed to be defending the Polish

Commonwealth from its enemies! Of course, there was another, a more cheerful, way of looking at his present circumstances. After all, this had to be how Winnetou and Old Chatterhand relieved themselves after imbibing copious amounts of firewater. So why shouldn't their devotee do the same? The urine came in fits and starts. When he was done and his trousers had been rebuttoned, he resumed his trek and, after taking one small step, noticed that his left pant leg was wet. One thing was quite certain. That wouldn't have happened had he been wearing leggings.

He stopped again near the skeletons and the now familiar smell of raw sewage. His family had lived in a villa near Łyczakow Cemetery in Lwów and he had liked to take long walks along the wooded, hilly, winding pathways of the old graveyard. Maria Konopnicka, his favorite poet, was buried there and, whenever he visited her grave, sometimes bringing flowers, sometimes a candle, he would recite his favorite patriotic poem:

> *Nie rzucim ziemi skąd nasz ród,*
> *Nie damy pogrześć mowy,*
> *Polski my naród, polski lud,*
> *Królewski szczep piastowy.*

He looked in Kortschenko's direction. The Ukrainian could not understand that a nation that would never abandon its land and never let its language be buried, that proudly asserted it was Polish and of royal origin, would never abandon Lwów. Of course, it made no difference to Poland what some unknown coffeehouse poet from Vienna did or did not believe. But it did make a difference to him. There were only two of them now and his own survival depended on Kortschenko's ability and willingness to forget his politics and cooperate with the enemy. The Ukrainian was sufficiently vain, amateurish, and cowardly not to pose too great a problem. Still, he had to be handled carefully—and cunningly. He had a stubborn streak and his *amour propre* had a tendency to assert itself at inconvenient moments. He was obviously concealing something about Golub's—and his own— traumatic encounter with the near-dead woman in the mound. Ultimately, it mattered little whether he, Pieracki, knew what that secret was. All that did matter was that the Ukrainian should *think* he knew.

Pieracki hobbled toward the window and decided to take a

look through the crack. The sudden exposure to bright light blinded him, but rapid blinking helped and he placed his eye back on the vertical line and peered out at the glassy white landscape. The snow had resumed falling and the wind was blowing. The crows had disappeared from the trees, presumably having found shelter in one of the dilapidated huts. The wavy surface of the snow glistened and sparkled and resembled what he imagined the ocean, on a hot windless day, must be like. Only the gulls and the smell of salt water were missing.

Incredibly, his thoughts turned to Karl May once again. Oh, how he had loved reading him as a boy and how disappointed he had been to discover that the German writer had never set foot in the Wild West. As to now, it was the dead of winter and he was snowbound and yet he distinctly felt like a paleface hiding from the Indians in, of all places, Death Valley. How curious that his mind should be playing tricks on him, reverting to his childhood instead of concentrating on the task at hand. Had his unconscious concluded that survival was unlikely and that the realm of fantasy was his only refuge?

*

Pieracki froze. There, in the distance, somewhat to the right and just barely visible behind the snowdrifts, were two dark figures or, more precisely, their bobbing heads and shoulders. He was certain. They weren't shadows. They weren't some kind of illusion. These were real human beings and not imaginary Indians. Pieracki held his breath as he hurried back to the table and crawled underneath. Kortschenko was still asleep. When he shook him awake, the Ukrainian opened one eye and gazed at him indifferently.

"I just saw someone outside," Pieracki said with a note of alarm.

"Who?"

"Two figures, off to the right—probably the same people you saw."

"I saw four or five."

Pieracki seized Kortschenko by the arm.

"Listen! Can you hear?"

"Yes." By now Kortschenko was fully awake. "Footsteps. Not far away."

"Are they coming in this direction?"

"Yes, I think so. They seem to be getting louder."

"They're definitely coming in this direction." Pieracki tightened his grip on Kortschenko's arm.

"Listen! Can you hear?"

Kortschenko nodded.

"We should hide in separate places. You stay here. I'll climb up on the oven."

"There's flesh on the skeletons," Pieracki declared. "The smell is terrible."

"If they find one of us, the other says nothing. *Einverstanden?*"

"*Tak*," Pieracki replied, "agreed."

As the Pole squeezed his body into the corner, raising his knees to his quivering lips and embracing them tightly with his arms, Kortschenko scuttled out from under the table. Conscious of resembling a minor character in some operetta, he crossed the room on tiptoe and with outstretched arms. Then he clambered onto the oven and, careful not to disturb the bones lest they crash to the floor, maneuvered himself between the skeletons and the icy wall. Four pairs of feet still bound in rags or clad in the remnants of shoes faced him. There were no rats or other vermin amid the bones, but the stench sickened him, far more so, curiously, than that of the mound. Lying flat on his stomach, Kortschenko turned his face to the wall and, with the tip of his nose grazing the clay, tried to inhale its earthen aroma.

Nothing could be gained from watching the doorway. It was even unnecessary to listen. If they were discovered, then their fate was in God's hands or, perhaps, in Stalin's. In any case, there was nothing they could do, but accept whatever lay in store. There was, he suddenly realized, a persuasive logic to passivity and fatalism. When there *really* was nothing to be done, when everything around you, when all of life militated against your continued existence, wasn't acquiescence in the will of God or in the brutal logic of human evil less pathetic, and perhaps even more noble, than resistance? The saints acquiesced in their persecution and death, not because they were cowards, but because they had a nobility of spirit that enabled them to ignore and transcend physical harm. He was certainly no saint, but perhaps the peasants were?

The crunching was distinctly audible now. Someone was

directly outside the hut. A gun went off—both Pieracki and Kortschenko tensed up—and the cawing of frightened crows and laughter followed. A man grunted loudly. Then there was a brief silence, a loud burp, and the sound of glass being smashed. The footsteps resumed. The man had entered the house and surveyed the antechamber. He sauntered into their room and waited, perhaps to acclimatize his eyes to the darkness, perhaps to determine whether the room housed any unusual smells. He took two steps. He saw the sickle lying on the table, took it, looked around, and left the room. Once he returned to the antechamber, they heard him unbuckle his pants and grunt. When the grunting finally stopped, they heard him adjust his clothes and shuffle out of the hut.

The crunching resumed. Someone shouted, but from a distance. Another gun was fired. And then, once again, there was silence. Pieracki and Kortschenko remained motionless, hardly breathing, and when the sense of imminent danger had passed, when both men felt they could resume normal breathing, they fell asleep.

*

They remained oblivious of the footsteps, the shots, and the yells all day. Whenever their eyes opened, they would stir and whimper and return to a deep slumber. After two hours, Pieracki fell over on his side and, with both hands serving as a pillow, slept on his shoulder. The ground was hard, but he felt nothing of the penetrating coldness anymore. Kortschenko remained lying with his face toward the wall, even when he turned over on his back. At one point, he felt a pressing need to urinate—it may have been real or it may have been a dream—and he decided, or dreamed he decided, to wet his pants. After all, climbing down was too difficult and, besides, it was quite unnecessary. The dead bodies next to him surely wouldn't mind the fresh urine of a living poet from Vienna.

It may have been the all-encompassing quiet of the approaching night that stirred Kortschenko from his slumber. He extended both arms in a yawn and realized, with only moderate disgust, that his right hand had plunged into a mass of bones and rags. He slid to the edge of the oven and, propping himself up with his good hand, dropped both feet over the side. His knees buckled as his feet touched the floor and he fell, face forward, onto the hard surface. Although his broken hand hadn't struck the ground, he felt an unexpectedly sharp stab in the palm of his right hand. It was the nail he had found in one of the huts. Kortschenko snorted at the absurdity of his hoping to defend himself with this tiny piece of metal. His colleagues in the Organization would have derided his pathetic interpretation of armed struggle. And they would have been right. What was a poet, and a coward, doing in the middle of the famine-stricken Ukrainian countryside? What chance did he have of organizing anything or anybody?

On second thought, even a modicum of cool reflection suggested that the fault was not entirely his own. *They* should have known better. After all, why did the Organization send *him*, a dandified denizen of the Café Central, on a difficult mission such as this? Wasn't the Pole right in saying the Organization was infiltrated by the Bolsheviks? And if it was, didn't that mean his mission had been planned in GPU headquarters in Moscow? That would certainly explain the ease with which they had captured him *and* the rapidity with which he had broken down and confessed. He had been a marked man. He was also absurd—he knew it—and his failure to realize in time just how absurd he was might kill him. But his experienced comrades, who should have known better, had been even more derelict. It was obvious that his current predicament was primarily *their* responsibility and *their* fault. He would gladly bear his share of the guilt—as long as they bore theirs and their share was significantly larger than his. *Was wahr ist, ist wahr:* what's true is true, after all.

Kortschenko crawled across the floor to the table, bumping his head against one of the legs. The sound awoke Pieracki.

"*Co?*" he cried. "Are they coming again?"

"It's time for us to go," Kortschenko said quietly, placing his hand on Pieracki's shoulder. "It's time for us to leave this morgue."

*

The cloud cover was as thin as an old silk scarf. The diffused light of the half-full moon cast a silvery glow that enabled the two men to make their way past the huts and orchards and apple trees, past the inky shadows and voices that, surprisingly, were silent on this night, and past the skeletal church, its crosses amputated, its walls smashed, its doors and windows broken, its bell lying forlornly in the snow. They came upon another graveyard, surrounded by a tilted iron fence, next to the church; amid the crosses and monuments there stood, in one corner, a small, irregularly shaped mound. The men knew they were bodies and this time they looked at them without horror or fear, hoping only not to notice any movement of stray limbs or broken heads that might engender in them too strong a sense of relief.

The road lay some one hundred meters beyond the church. It was narrow, about the same width as the road on which they had been transported two days ago in the van, and it was covered with tightly packed snow, with tire ruts running along both sides. It was obviously a well-traveled artery that led somewhere. Just as obviously, it would be patrolled and they would have to be vigilant in order to avoid capture. There was also the possibility that they might encounter fleeing peasants or bands of marauders. The former might help them; the latter would certainly attempt to kill them. Flight was impossible; so, too, was resistance. The ubiquitous whiteness would have to serve as the ersatz table under which they could hide.

The snow sloped down from the embankments on both left and right. It had acquired a hauntingly bluish glow that accentuated the purple shadows and endowed the ruts with a breadth and depth they did not have. The road stretched out like a long pier that extended into the mist and, ultimately, the sea. There was nothing to be heard, except for an occasional gust of tired wind and the sound of their shoes crushing particles of ice. After days in bleak cells, suffocating vans, decaying huts, and waste-high snow, the sensation of an open road struck both men as unnatural and, instead of an exhilarating sense of freedom, they felt unease, anxiety, and trepidation. Neither man regretted abandoning the dreadful confinement that had pressed down upon him like a metal vise, but neither knew how to react to the vistas that had opened up before them. It was as if they had taken a wrong turn and were now hopelessly lost in the middle of a vast field.

They advanced deliberately, careful to avoid stepping into ruts and twisting an ankle or falling and listening for suspicious noises, their eyes cast downward, their faces covered with cold sweat, their weakened bodies desperately desirous of sleep. Kortschenko held the nail in his right hand, squeezing it tightly in order to stay awake. Pieracki carried the rod he had found in one of the huts. His knee had begun throbbing again and he leaned against the staff every few paces and rested.

"I need to sit down."

"Let's go beyond that bend." Kortschenko crossed the road and took Pieracki by the arm. "Can you make it?"

They went on for another hundred meters and, after the road curved slightly to the right, collapsed near an embankment. Pieracki released a pitiful groan and straightened out his right leg. Kortschenko scooped up a handful of snow and pressed it to his face and mouth, waiting for it to melt before he extended his tongue. The snow had a pleasantly sweet taste, which he recognized but could not place. Was it milk? Fresh raspberries? Or the vanilla sauce on a warm piece of Strudel at Heiner's? Pieracki moaned again, as he leaned back and let his head sink into the snow.

"Don't lie down," Kortschenko admonished him. "If we fall asleep, we're—"

"—dead. I know. Just for a second. *Proszę.* I need to stretch my back."

"Can you walk?"

"Yes. I'll be fine in a minute."

As Pieracki finished speaking, the sound of a motor, coughing like an asthmatic, reached them. Headlights flashed and lit the ghostly mist somewhere in the distance. Pieracki swore— "*Kurwa!*"—and, turning onto his stomach, burrowed into the snow. Kortschenko followed him. The vehicle approached, slowed down as it came into the curve, and resumed speed. The men heard it rattle by. After another minute, the choking sound drifted away. The Ukrainian raised his head above the snow. Everything was black and there was no sign of the headlights. He looked at the sky and noticed that the moon, fortunately, had hidden behind a cloud. The Pole's blond head appeared.

"What time do you think it is? How much more of this damned night is there?"

"Probably after midnight." Kortschenko brushed the snow from his hair. "Let's hope it doesn't snow. We should be fine, as long as it doesn't snow."

Getting to their feet was difficult for both men. The snow was deep, their footing was uncertain, and they were weak.

Kortschenko had to maneuver himself onto his knees and, only after squatting and extending his good arm in the manner of a Cossack dancer utterly lacking in poise, was he able to straighten himself out. Pieracki watched with a bemused expression on his face and held out his hand. Once the Pole was standing, Kortschenko gave him the staff. Both men held it tightly, their heads and hands touching, almost as if they were monks in silent prayer. They breathed deeply and listened to their hearts calm down and the pounding in their heads abate.

*

The sun rose almost directly behind them and Pieracki and Kortschenko were heartened to see that they were, as they had hoped, actually walking westwards. The sky ahead remained a dark and listless gray, but the sun illuminated the embankments before them with a bright ochre glow. The obsidian-colored snow turned charcoal and then, after five or ten minutes, white and blue and green, with glistening patches of gold. The land on both sides of the road was perfectly even, punctuated only by clumps of barren trees, slender rises that could have been hills or snowdrifts or mounds of corpses, and, from time to time, the sooty swaths of distant woods. Crows circled above them, emitting shrieks that echoed eerily in the emptiness of the landscape.

A cluster of gloomy huts came into view near the horizon to their left. No smoke was wafting from the chimneys. Nor was there any trace of a road leading to the huts. They considered wading through the deep snow, but decided it would be pointless. The settlement would be inhabited only by corpses; they were certain not to find any food; and the strain of walking in waist-high snow would drain them of their last drop of energy. Two more days without food—or hope—would very likely end in a miserable death under some miserable table in some miserable hut.

It was after the settlement vanished behind a clump of pine trees that they first noticed the mounds along the road. They were bodies, of course, and for all they knew the dead had lined the road for the entire time they had walked throughout the night. But now, with the sun occasionally peeking through the blotted clouds, they could see the unmistakable signs of a mass migration to extermination. The neatly rounded, snow-covered mounds resembled large ant hills. Every once in a while, a stray hand or finger or head or foot disrupted the symmetry. Most of the bodies appeared to be well preserved—very much like the young girl they had encountered in the stream—with only the exposed parts evincing signs of advanced rot. Curiously, women and children predominated. Where were the men? Had they died fighting? Had they been shipped off to Siberia? Or had they fallen into despair more easily and given up? The children were of all ages; only infants appeared to be missing. Were they stillborn and buried or simply unborn? Or, Kortschenko shuddered as he recalled Kateryna Fedorivna, had their soft flesh been devoured by starving parents?

"We have passed one hundred and forty-eight corpses," Pieracki said after an hour. "Where could they have been going, *mon ami?*"

"Look," Kortschenko pointed to a large pile on the left. "An entire family!"

"Is no one alive here?" Pieracki exclaimed. "Is this entire country dead?" He leaned on his staff and looked genuinely anguished.

"How could they all die? It is physically impossible for everyone to die." His voice turned strident, like that of a street preacher imploring the world to end its evil ways before it was too late.

"How can that be? Tell me, Pan Kortschenko, how can that possibly be?"

"I don't know."

Pieracki seized Kortschenko by the arm. "Do you know what gives me no peace, *mon ami?*"

"What?"

"How could they all just *accept* death?"

It occurred to Kortschenko that, perhaps for the first time in his life, he actually had an answer to a question about life, one that qualified as intrinsically *lebenswichtig* and possibly had important implications for his own existence.

"They knew there was no alternative," he pronounced. "They knew their destruction had been planned and that there was no escape." He shrugged.

"Where can you go and what can you do if you have nowhere to go and nothing to do? They retained their dignity, didn't they? And now they're at peace, aren't they?"

"*Tak, ja wiem*—I know. I understand that perfectly, *mon ami*. And still, I confess, I do not understand at all—*w ogóle nie*." Pieracki shook his head vigorously.

"Well, at least the Bolsheviks are living like kings."

"Except for our poor friend, Golub. The fool remained a believer to the end."

"He was beginning to waver"—Kortschenko's voice dropped—"after he strangled that woman in the graveyard." He coughed and raised his hand to his mouth.

"That experience shattered him. It would have shattered me—or anyone, for that matter."

Pieracki gave Kortschenko a penetrating glance.

"Couldn't you have stopped him, *mon ami*?"

The Pole was about to say more, to ask the question that gave him no peace, but then, after catching sight of a small hand, its flesh putrid and black, protruding from the snow at his feet, he sighed. The questions really didn't matter. Nothing really mattered.

"*That* is why I joined the Organization," the Ukrainian said after seeing Pieracki's tell-tale glance, "to *destroy* this."

As Kortschenko made a wide arc with his good hand, an irrepressible desire to burst out giggling overcame the Pole.

"I think that you—and I—have lost the battle, Pan Kortschenko. It is *we* who are being destroyed!"

Kortschenko remained silent. Then, quietly, he said, "Let's go," and resumed walking. A few seconds later, he turned to Pieracki.

"I am just a poet and not a very good one at that," he said bitterly. "Why should I win battles? Even the brave poets, like Byron, died. So why should the cowards live?" He looked at the ground and rubbed his eyes.

"The glare is blinding me. This—all of this, all of this—is too much for me, too much."

*

The sky was still blue and the sun was shining intensely as they came upon a straight length of road that extended outward like a string and disappeared at the horizon. The snow banks gleamed with a shocking brilliance, like piles of rock salt, and the glare forced the men to hold their hands over their eyes and squint. Recalling the imaginary expanses of Lwów, where he and his brother had mounted camels, embarked on arduous campaigns against the heathen, and prayed for a shimmering oasis to appear, Pieracki held his breath as he realized that this was what a real desert had to look like. He laughed at himself. First, it was Karl May and the memories of the kitchen table; now, it was Rudyard Kipling. Since when did Polish gentlemen-spies recall their boyhood with such clarity? However amusing, all these irrepressible memories were beginning to disturb him. Could it be that they heralded the beginning of the end? And who was next— Sherlock Holmes?

His deliberations came to an abrupt end when Kortschenko stopped in his tracks and, jabbing at the sky with his right forefinger, excitedly cried:

"Look, Pan Pieracki! *There!* A house! A house! And there is smoke!"

"Where, *mon ami*, where?"

"There! There! *See it?*"

"No, no, I don't think so." Pieracki leaned the staff against his chest and shielded his eyes from the sun with both hands.

"It's just up ahead—*there!* On the embankment! Right by the road!"

Pieracki squinted. The light and shadows danced before his eyes.

"Yes, yes, I think I see it now. Yes, I think I see it. Perhaps they can shelter us."

"And give us food," Kortschenko said. "Of course, they'll feed us—with honey. And milk—they'll give us milk—as much as we can drink!"

Kortschenko ran ahead, waving his arms, shouting, and smacking his lips like a madman. Pieracki placed the staff in front of him as far as he dared and followed with short quick steps. The Ukrainian reached the embankment and began climbing it, grasping at the hardened, glittering snow with his trembling hands. He reached the top and—just as Pieracki's cry, "Is anyone there?" reached him—found nothing but snow and an endlessly level landscape that stretched out, barren and empty, in all directions.

"Where is it?" Pieracki said as he neared Kortschenko. "The house—where is it?"

The Ukrainian was standing quite still, with his sullen face lowered to the ground.

"There is no house," Kortschenko replied flatly. "It was an illusion—a mirage, a *fata morgana*. There is nothing here, absolutely nothing." He looked around with a look of despair on his face.

"And yet I saw it so clearly, so very clearly. How can it not be here?"

He had intended to kiss the ground and embrace the peasants who would have greeted him with bread and salt, a long-lost son come back from his endless wanderings. Instead, there was nothing—nothing but snow. The damned whiteness was blinding him and confusing his senses. No, it was worse than that: he was drowning in it. He was suffocating in its implacable embrace. This was the end—*das Ende*.

"Come down," Pieracki said softly. "I saw it, too. Hunger can play tricks on us. We were both hallucinating. Come down, Pan Kortschenko. We have to keep going. Come down, *mon ami*, come down."

Kortschenko raised his head and shouted defiantly: "Come down? *Why?* Why come down? *Wozu?*" He folded his arms across his chest.

"We will die, Pan Pieracki, we will die. I know that for certain: we will die. *Ja, wir werden sterben*. In the middle of this emptiness—in the middle of this accursed whiteness. *Jawohl, wir werden sterben*." Kortschenko dropped both arms to his sides.

"And what difference does it make whether we die here or elsewhere? Tell me, Pan Pieracki: what difference does it make?" He glared fiercely at the Pole, who stared back.

"I have no strength anymore, Pan Pieracki. I need to sleep."

"Come," the Pole said, extending his hand to Kortschenko. "If we keep walking west, we'll reach the Zbrucz. The peasants will give us shelter. The Ukrainians will take us in. They are kind and good people. You said so yourself, *mon ami*. The famine cannot be everywhere. We just need to keep walking. Please, *mon ami*, come down—come."

As Kortschenko slid down the embankment, Pieracki continued breathlessly.

"What will you do when you get home, *mon ami?* Tell me. *Moi*, I intend to take a bath—a long, hot bath. And then, after I shave, I will go dancing in the evening, perhaps with Jadwiga or perhaps with Janina, or maybe with both. *Tak*, I'll take them both.

Have I ever told you about Jadwiga and Janina? Beautiful girls, *bardzo piękne*, blondes, both of them. Coquettes. They could be Parisian. Yes, *mon ami*, they could be Parisian. They love champagne, they love French underclothes, and they never say *non*. *Vous comprenez?*"

Kortschenko took a deep breath and resumed walking.

"No, *mon ami*, I've made up my mind. I know exactly what I'll do. First, billiards at the club with my friends, Wojtek and Tadek. Excellent chaps, perhaps someday I'll introduce you. And *wódka*, oceans of *wódka*. Yes, first the friends and the billiards and the *wódka*—and then the girls. After all, I'll need nourishment, won't I? And I'll need to avoid solids. And Jadwiga and Janina can wait. After all, I won't have the strength, will I?" Pieracki forced a laugh.

"And you, my friend, what will you do?"

"Shoot a Russian communist," Kortschenko said grimly.

"How serious of you, *mon ami!* Straight to work! You nationalists must learn to enjoy life—to live. *Trzeba żyć!*"

"I will enjoy watching him die."

"How morbid of you, *mon ami!* You can do better. Come, you can do better."

"And then I'll go to a wine garden in Grinzing and have a liter of young wine."

"Well, now *that* is more like it! That is *much* better. And you will dance with the *Wiener Mäderl?*"

"I will dance with every girl."

"And you will kiss them?"

"*Selbstverständlich.*"

"See, my friend? *Tout va bien.* All is well and all will be well. We must just keep walking. Soon, very soon, we will be home. I can feel it in my bones. And you, *mon ami*—can you feel it in your bones, too?"

*

For the first time since their captivity, the cloudless sky was a glorious blue and the golden sun beat down on them mercilessly. The metallic snow glowed with a painful intensity and they had to walk with their heads cast downward and their eyes half-closed. Crows flew overhead and at one point a large white bird, its wings outstretched, glided elegantly over the fields to their left.

Kortschenko watched it disappear beyond the horizon. Was it an omen? And, if so, what did it portend? Nervous puddles of water appeared in the road and they soon found themselves negotiating patches of sodden earth that was not quite mud, but sufficiently mud-like to make walking onerous. They unbuttoned their coats and loosened their collars and felt the perspiration run down their necks and backs in steady streams. Their putrid bodies stank of waste and the foul fumes they released were a grim reminder of their own essential incompatibility with the crystalline beauty of their surroundings.

The snow grew soft and porous from the warmth, exposing more of the corpses lying underneath. They came upon the small body of a young boy, certainly no more than eleven or twelve, lying on his back with both arms stretched out stiffly at his sides. Crows were pecking at his lips and eyes and Pieracki tried to shoo them away with his staff. They flapped their wings distractedly and withdrew, but, once the men passed, they returned with renewed vigor. Some forty meters down the road, the men saw the fully exposed bodies of a woman, her face sunk in the lumpy mud, her hands tied with barbed wire, and a bald man, who lay on his back, disemboweled, his intestines exposed and rotting and full of vermin, with a gaggle of pitch-black crows gathered about him.

Men were still in the minority and children were still overrepresented. Most had bloated bellies and sunken cheeks and stick-like arms and legs that had been reduced to yellow-gray skin and sharply protruding bones. Where olive-green grass peeked out from beneath the patches of snow, the bodies looked like they were resting in a park or playground or near a river or lake. The stench had become overpowering, just as the dead driver had predicted. Pieracki and Kortschenko focused their eyes on the ruts and gullies and puddles in the road. They were terrified to look and to speak and indifferent to what they would see and could say.

As they climbed a small incline in the road, their trance-like concentration was interrupted by the sound of a tin voice. It belonged to a man who was half-sitting, half-lying on the side of the road in the mud. He was bearded and wet, from head to toe, and he wore rags on the skeletal remains of his body. His long black hair fell in thick knotted strands into his yellow face. His glassy eyes looked out from beneath thick eyebrows made to look thicker by the thinness of his face and body. His lips were pulled back, revealing two rows of rotting brown teeth. He had, evidently, collapsed no more than one or two days ago and had managed to stay alive despite—or perhaps because of—the snow cover.

"*A Vy khto?*" Kortschenko asked hesitantly in Ukrainian. "Who are you?"

"Bread," the man replied weakly. "*Mayete khliba?*"

"How can we have bread?" Kortschenko wanted to laugh. "Are you from here?"

The man nodded.

"Where are we?"

"Ukraina," the man said.

"Yes, we know," Pieracki said. "But where?"

"Stepanivka."

"Your village?"

The man nodded.

"Where is Kyiv?"

The man motioned with his head.

"And Kharkiv?"

He smiled and said, "Bread."

"We have nothing, my friend," Kortschenko said. "Can you walk?"

The man appeared to shake his head.

"We cannot stay with you."

Again, the man smiled.

"Is Stepanivka far?"

The man shook his head.

"Is anyone still alive—in Stepanivka?"

"*Ni.*"

Kortschenko looked at Pieracki and raised his eyebrows. The Pole motioned ahead with his hand.

"We can barely drag our own bodies. How can we possibly take him along?"

"But if we leave him, he will die."

"And if we take him, *we* will die."

Kortschenko turned to the man. He wanted to apologize, to beg his forgiveness for a crime, a sin, he did not commit, to prostrate himself at his feet.

Instead, he said, "We cannot take you with us."

The man said nothing.

"You will have to manage on your own here. Will you manage?" Kortschenko sensed that, if he didn't end the conversation immediately, he would soon be imploring a dead man for mercy.

The man raised his eyes to the sky and said, "The snow..."

"What about the snow?"

"It melted."

"Yes, it's warmer."

"Unfortunately."

"Why?"

"I am"—the man's lips flared into something resembling a grin—"alive."

"It will come down again," Kortschenko said soothingly. "Soon. I am sure."

"Pray that it does."

"And we will pray for you," Pieracki added.

"And I"—the man lay back in the snow—"for you."

"Come, *mon ami.*" Pieracki tugged at Kortschenko's sleeve. "There is nothing we can do for him. Let him die in peace. Let him join his country."

*

It was at noon, when the sun hung high like a bright orange orb in the cloudless azure sky, that they heard an increasingly loud rumbling behind them. It had to be a truck, perhaps even a convoy, and it couldn't have been more than three hundred meters away. They looked about frantically, searching for a hiding place, but there was nothing in the depthless landscape except for the snowdrifts and the corpses along the road.

Kortschenko stared at the piles.

"I cannot—*nein. Ich kann nicht.* You go there if you want to. I'll climb into the snow."

"But they will see your tracks!"

"I cannot—not again. You must forgive me, you must understand. I cannot, I simply cannot."

The Pole burrowed into a mound of corpses on the right side of the road, while the Ukrainian crawled into a snowdrift on the left. No more than a half minute later, the first truck appeared from behind the bend. It was a military vehicle and in the back sat two rows of red-cheeked soldiers, their fur hats lowered over their foreheads, their rifles rattling at their sides. Then another truck lumbered along, with the same two rows of sullen young soldiers in the back. Finally, there came a third. It decelerated just after it passed the two men, coughed, and came to a grinding halt. Someone barked a command and the soldiers clambered down and went up to the snowdrifts and mounds and relieved themselves. Another bark followed and the soldiers scampered back; after several fitful starts, the truck resumed its journey.

Pieracki was clutching his right knee as he emerged from under the pile of dead bodies. He had struck it against a bone and the excruciating pain had shot through his right side. He called out to Kortschenko—the soles of his shoes were visible in the snow and it was a miracle that he hadn't been seen—but the Ukrainian failed to respond. Pieracki stumbled across the road and tapped Kortschenko's foot with his staff. He remained motionless. Pieracki then plunged the staff into the snow. The Ukrainian groaned, curved his back like a cat, and gradually lifted his head.

"I fell asleep." Kortschenko frowned. "Can you believe that? The snow felt like a down comforter. I even began dreaming. Can you believe that? I was at home and it was a celebration of some kind, a birthday or Easter. All our friends were there and the table was covered with food and drink. My mother had baked a *Schwarzwälderkirschtorte* and my father was pontificating in the smoking room." He rose to his feet.

"I hurt my knee again," Pieracki announced.

"Can you walk?"

"Yes, but I need to rest."

"Let's go a little farther." Kortschenko brushed the debris off his sleeves. "Where there are no dead bodies."

After thirty minutes they found a small earthen hollow in the embankment that could also shelter them from the burning sun. Pieracki dropped to the ground and extended his leg. His knee was throbbing, but the pain was manageable and would probably subside in a minute or two. Kortschenko checked the snow for bodies and, finding none, plunged his fist into it. He withdrew a handful and drank it in eagerly. Once again, he was struck by its curiously pleasant, and seemingly familiar, taste. Was it *Apfelstrudel?* A Kracherl? As his head sank against the moist brown earth, something tickled his neck. It was a tiny insect.

"Eat it," Pieracki suggested. "Not quite the Sacher, but

edible."

"You cannot be serious!"

"We ate bugs when I was in the army. We trained in the swamps of Polesie—a terrible place, by the way, much worse than this," Pieracki replied. "In some countries, they are considered delicacies." He caught one crawling along his pant leg.

"See?" He squashed it and popped it into his mouth.

Kortschenko contorted his face and placed the dead bug on the tip of his outstretched tongue. He then retracted it and swallowed.

"You will survive." Pieracki tapped him on his shoulder. "Besides, our stomachs couldn't digest anything larger than a bug. See? It has no taste." He grinned weakly.

"Alas, *mon ami*, we shall live to see another day."

After consuming five or six insects, the two men sat back, exhausted and out of breath. The mud had seeped into their clothes, inducing a sense of calm similar to what one might feel upon immersing oneself in a bathtub. They exchanged some words about the impermissibility of falling asleep and promptly fell asleep, but only briefly, for fewer than fifteen minutes. A cloud cover, as impermeable and gray as in past days, had advanced rapidly across the sky and obliterated the sun. The temperature dropped precipitously and the wind began blowing so hard as to whip up and scatter pieces of wet snow. The men shivered in the frigid mud and the chattering of their teeth awoke them. It was early afternoon and they knew that the sun would set in another two or three hours.

*

The slush and snow hardened rapidly, as did the puddles in the road and the mud. The wind picked up and a thin, prickly snow that hurt the skin and stung the eyes began dropping from the angry sky. As they were coming down a small incline, Kortschenko slipped and tried to break the fall with his left hand. The pain felt like a branding iron and he turned over on his side, like a wounded animal. Pieracki watched silently, unable to do anything but wait. The sight of the helpless Kortschenko struggling with the mud and ice only underscored what he knew all too well: that their situation was both serious *and* hopeless.

And then, inexplicably, Pieracki recalled Golub's ridiculous rendition of some baseball song. The Jew was right. What else was one to do in the face of unremitting hopelessness but sing a popular American tune that sniggered at the meaninglessness of existence by celebrating absurdity? He had liked the song so much that he had even bought the record and played it incessantly on his parents' Victrola:

> Yes, we have no bananas,
> We have no bananas today.
> We've string beans, and onions
> Cabashes, and scallions,
> And all sorts of fruit and say

"You're as *meshugge* as the Jew," Kortschenko muttered, as he finally got to his feet and looked around. He placed his finger on his lips, but the Pole ignored him and continued at the top of his voice:

> We have an old fashioned tomato
> A Long Island potato
> But yes, we have no bananas
> We have no bananas today.

"And besides," Pieracki added when he had finished, "they can't hear anything but their own motors in those damned trucks."

The Pole had a point. Wasn't this Ukraine and weren't Ukrainians known for their singing? Wasn't the land supposed to resound with melodies? Didn't the singing testify to the land's vitality and life? Wasn't that why Kateryna Fedorivna sang as she died? As he recalled their earlier rendition of "*Wien, Wien, nur du allein*"—oh, how long ago that had been!—Kortschenko raised a hand to his throat, almost as if he were checking the fitness of his vocal chords, and whistled a tune from some Viennese operetta.

"Kálmán?" Pieracki asked.

"Yes, *Gräfin Mariza*."

"One of my favorites. I actually saw it at the Volksoper two years ago."

"I prefer *Die Csárdásfürstin*," Kortschenko replied, "but I've never been able to remember those Magyar melodies."

Pieracki frowned.

"Do not trust the Hungarians, *mon ami*. They desire a greater Hungary. It is in their blood. Why don't they take an example from you Austrians? You lost an empire, but what difference does it make when you still have *Schlag* and the Kaiserball?"

None at all, Kortschenko wanted to say, none at all. There was no point in engaging the uncharacteristically serious and still slippery Pole. He had had it up to here with politics and, moreover, his amusing Magyars friends cared far more about wine, women, and song than about revanchist dreams of empire. No, it would be best to sing and he knew just what: the refrain from *"Wiener Blut."*

> *Willkommen*
> *In der Dunkelheit*
> *In der Dunkelheit*

"Ah, the incomparable Strauss!" Pieracki remarked gaily and, suddenly smiling, joined Kortschenko.

> *In der Einsamkeit*
> *In der Traurigkeit*
> *Für die Ewigkeit*

Before the final notes had been sung, however, Pieracki's mood turned somber again.

"Darkness, loneliness, sadness forever," he said. "I had never paid attention to the words before. Ironic, isn't it? You Viennese belong here—in this hopeless land. Yes, *mon ami*, you Viennese are Ukrainians. Most of you will die, but some of you will survive, at least until 1683 returns and the next barbarians come. And then it will be up to you to sacrifice yourselves for the civilized world again."

*

The lengthening shadows announced that it would soon be dark and they knew that another night spent in the cold air of the black Ukrainian steppes might prove fatal. As they considered their choices and decided they had none, they encountered the first fork in the road since they began their journey. The road with the ruts veered off to the left. To the right was a far narrower track, just wide enough to accommodate a cart or a wagon and, as the absence of tire tracks seemed to attest, evidently untraveled.

"Let's follow the main road. We'll have a better chance of finding a village, of finding shelter."

"But that road goes *east*," Pieracki responded emphatically, "and we want to go *west*." He pointed past the narrow track leading to the right.

"And if we find nothing? We could freeze to death."

"And if we go left, the soldiers could find us."

"Not if we find a village first."

"Filled with corpses and cannibals? *Merçi beaucoup, mon ami*, I think I prefer the cold night air and the possibility of freezing."

They stood at the crossroads and turned their heads uncertainly in both directions. The sky on the left was a mixture of charcoal, blue, and purple tones. That on the right was purple, red, and yellow. The road to the left went straight for a hundred meters and then disappeared behind a small knoll. The road to the right curved immediately behind a group of tall pine trees.

"Have you wondered," Kortschenko mused, "why the GPU has not found us?"

"Perhaps they're not even looking."

"But we're escaped politicals!"

"We're insignificant, *mon ami*. A communist fool, a Viennese poet, a German aristocrat, and a Polish spy with torn pants: what have they to fear from us? Why send a search party when the snow will do the job for them?"

"You were more optimistic before, Pan Pieracki."

"Oh, I still am, *mon ami*, I still am. But my optimism is grounded in realism. We Poles are romantics, but some of us are not entirely blind."

"Are you sure that road leads west?"

"Of course," Pieracki replied. "*There*, see? There's the sun. It will probably set in an hour or so. If we walk westwards, at least we know we're headed for Poland. If we go east, well—there's nothing there, only death and more death and still more death. And Russia. Surely you don't want to go to Russia?"

Kortschenko smiled back. "Very well, Pan Pieracki, you win: we go west." He then added, as an afterthought, "And may the Lord be with us."

"Oh, *mon ami*, the good Lord abandoned us long ago! But I suspect that God, if He exists on this Earth, resides in the West: in the mountains of Switzerland, perhaps, or on the Côte d'Azur. He will be glad that we are rejoining him, like two prodigal sons. And then, after we share a Schnapps and a *Sachertorte* with Him and say an Our Father in Saint Stephen's, He will not, I am sure, abandon us again."

*

The track was far more uneven than the road and walking proved exceedingly arduous, especially for the limping Pieracki. The countryside began to change its appearance as well. The flatness of the landscape was replaced by gentle inclines that hinted at hills. Clusters of trees appeared, some quite close, some distant and seemingly as solid and thick as woods. The sky was almost uniformly gray, a thick sheet of slate, but with their skilled eyes they were able to discern a barely perceptible lightness up ahead.

"See?" Pieracki joked. "Even the terrain is beginning to resemble Galicia. I tell you, *mon ami*, we made the right decision. Soon we shall be sitting in a sauna drinking Kirschwasser!"

"Why are there no corpses along the road?" Kortschenko asked suspiciously. "Why have the dead bodies disappeared? How can that be? There should be corpses here."

"But that's good, isn't it? Why should two half-corpses want corpses?"

"I'm not joking," Kortschenko said. "*Das war kein Schmäh.* If there are no bodies here, then there are no people here—and no villages."

"Or just the opposite," Pieracki countered. "Perhaps there are no bodies here because the peasants are safely at home, guzzling *wódka*, bouncing their babies on their knees, and making love."

"I have a foreboding, Pan Pieracki. *Ich sehe schwarz.*"

"A foreboding? Of what? No, *mon ami*, we must go west," Pieracki said resolutely. "There is no alternative. You know that. And besides, we have had forebodings every day. What difference does this one make?"

The sky before them had acquired a faintly reddish hue, like a washed out blood stain on a handkerchief. Large snowflakes glided lazily to the ground, until the wind swept them up and sent them flying in all directions. The track narrowed and the men walked side by side, occasionally brushing against each other. Both were breathing heavily and dragging their feet. Neither was whistling or singing. It was time to rest and to sleep.

In the distance, beyond some darkened trees, but clearly

silhouetted against the sky, protruded an unmistakable onion-shaped dome. The church, a small wooden structure with a slanted roof, soon came into view. As they approached it, they could see that the cross had been severed and the bell tower had been dismantled. The bell was missing, presumably molten down for machine parts or ammunition. Two neat rows of huts, their windows, doors, and thatched roofs intact, were arrayed along the top of a rise and extended to the left and to the right of the church. There was no light, no smell of smoke, no sound. Except for the elongated purple shadows, the village was empty, abandoned even by cannibals.

"We will be safe here," Pieracki said hopefully.
Once again, his thoughts drifted, irrepressibly and unaccountably, to the Wild West, where Old Chatterhand and Winnetou crept through the sage brush, their guns cocked, their brows knitted in eager anticipation of a big fight. This time, he would be Winnetou and the Ukrainian could be Old Chatterhand and, after painted braves hurtled their tomahawks and missed their heads by millimeters, they would emerge victorious and slap each other cheerfully on the back.

*

As they neared the huts, they encountered a nauseating smell far more intense than anything they had experienced before. The huts had to be full of rotting bodies. There was no other explanation. For whatever reason, perhaps because they were so isolated or perhaps because they felt they were safe, the inhabitants of the settlement must have decided against fleeing. They lay in their huts—sprawled out on the ovens, on the tables, on their trunks, on the floor—sheltered from the ice and snow and cold by the roofs and doors and windows, where they had been rotting for weeks, possibly even months. The vermin had probably feasted on their decaying and decomposing corpses and multiplied with abandon. This was hell, Kortschenko thought, a charnel house that promised annihilation for anyone who entered it.

The two men held their noses as they approached the hut nearest the church. As the Ukrainian pulled open the roughly hewn wooden door, they were greeted by the nervous scurrying of scores of filthy mice and even filthier rats and an overwhelming odor of putrefaction that made them gulp instinctively and cover their mouths. Kortschenko slammed shut the door and spat out a large glob of phlegm.

"*Ich kann nicht*," he declared. "I cannot go inside. These huts are slaughterhouses. I cannot."

"The church," Pieracki suggested. "Let's try the church."

A board was nailed across the door and it took them close to fifteen minutes to pry it loose. The setting sun cast a dim light on the interior. It was empty and no sounds of vermin greeted them. Four meters away stood the iconostasis, its gold frames glistening darkly and its painted icons almost invisible to the eye. Hanging from the three crosses, evenly arrayed along the top of the iconostasis, were three emaciated bodies. The nooses had been attached to the crosses. The central figure, with long white hair and a long white beard and dressed in a black cassock, was obviously the village priest. The other two were probably village elders or kulaks. Their heads were tilted to the sides, their glassy eyes bulged, as if they were surprised by their own death, and their blackened tongues extended from their distorted mouths to their pointy chins. Their hands were tied behind their backs and their bare feet, bloody and swollen, dangled below. Pieracki stepped back in horror. Kortschenko shut his eyes and turned on his heels. There was no question of spending the night in this terrible place. They slammed the door, crossed themselves, and stepped away from the building.

"*Matko Boska*" is all Pieracki could say. It occurred to him that those were among the first words he had uttered upon being thrown into the cell so very, very long ago. He had, evidently, come full circle.

"What do we do now, Pan Pieracki?" Kortschenko implored. "What can we do now? We need rest. Where are we to go? Tell me, Pan Pieracki, where are we to go?"

"West—that is all we can do. There's a bluff of some kind just beyond the huts. Perhaps there's another settlement farther away."

Pieracki spoke without conviction and Kortschenko knew it. The Pole was right, of course: they had to go west. Where else were they to go? But would they find another settlement? Would it be habitable? Or would the smell of death haunt them wherever their muddy legs took them?

*

They struggled up the escarpment, mounted the hill, and surveyed the vast expanse before them. It was a river, frozen solid and covered with seemingly undulating waves of white and blue snow. They could see the sun set beyond it.

"It's the Dnipro," Kortschenko said despondently. "Do you see how wide it is? We'll never cross it. We'll never reach the Polish border. It's hopeless, Pan Pieracki. It's the end. *Kaputt*—we are *kaputt*."

Pieracki looked about furtively, silently, as if he were making a decision.

"Come, let's go!" he suddenly shouted. "We can walk across and then we will keep walking until we reach the Zbrucz!"

"You can hardly stand." Kortschenko spoke quietly, but with firmness. "The river is covered with ice and there's a strong wind. You will fall, Pan Pieracki. You will break a leg or an arm. And it will be dark before you get to the other side. Or you could turn upstream or downstream in the mist and never reach the shore. And what if the ice cracks? It is madness, Pan Pieracki, it is suicide. Let's wait until tomorrow. We will have all day to cross."

"Are you coming?" Pieracki asked. He began hobbling down the hill.

"Are you coming? I will not wait. I cannot wait, *mon ami*. We must go, we must go, we must go home, *mon ami*—now, now! Are you coming? I must go home, I must go home. Home, *mon ami*, home! They are waiting for me at home! We must go, *mon ami*. Are you coming?"

"Go, then." Kortschenko spoke to no one, as the Pole was already out of earshot. "*Do widzenia*, Pan Pieracki. And don't forget that Lwów is ours!"

He watched the Pole lower himself from the embankment onto the frozen river. Pieracki walked slowly, carefully planting his feet on the snow-covered ice. The wind had grown stronger and the snow flurries increased. He made his way uncertainly, pausing frequently, adjusting his clothes, sheltering his face from the biting wind, and increasingly relying on his staff for support. After half an hour, Kortschenko could see only his wobbly outline, a shadow amid the swirling snowflakes and the thickening mist. He kept watching until the shadow disappeared. Had the Pole fallen? Was he still walking? Did he know where he was going? Would he freeze in the middle of the river?

All at once the Ukrainian cried, "Pan Pieracki! Pan Pieracki! Come back! It is madness. You will get nowhere, Pan Pieracki! Come back! Come back! It is madness. Come back!"

*

The shadow did not return. Nor was there any sound, except for the lugubrious howling of the wind. Could the Pole even hear him? Could anyone hear him? There was no one here. There was nothing here. Everything was dead, rotten, and decaying and everyone was dead, rotten, and decaying. Ukraine—*his* Ukraine—was dead, a corpse. No, it was worse. It was gone. It had disappeared, vanished. It had been extinguished and obliterated by the Russians. And all that remained was an indistinct memory, a tune or two, and some bad poetry to remind him that the object of his dreams had once been a real country with real people.

> Yes, we have no bananas,
> We have no bananas today.

He shut his eyes and lay back. At least here, on the side of the hill, there was no stench. He had to rest; he had to decide what he was going to do. He had to get to Vienna.

> *Wien, Wien, nur du allein,*
> *Sollst stets die Stadt meiner Träume sein!*

He had to find his table in the Café Central. He had to order an espresso. He had to write a poem or, if the Muse struck him, two. He had to flirt with the girls and go to the Opernball. He had to have a *Nusstorte* at Demel's and a *Liptauerbrot* at the Esterhazy and a liter at the Urbani. He had to listen to *Die Csárdásfürstin* at the Volksoper. He had so many things to do. And then—then he would resume the struggle against Russian imperialism and return to save Kateryna Fedorivna and the old man from Stepanivka and sing and sing and sing and liberate this land—*his* land.

> *Ya kazala u vivtorok*
> *potsiluyu raziv sorok,*
> *ty pryyshov mene nema*
> *pidmanula pidvela.*

Everything would be clear. Everything would fall into

place. Ukraine would finally be free. All would be forgotten and forgiven. He would be clean again. Victory was inevitable.

Willkommen
In der Dunkelheit

His head sank slowly into the whiteness surrounding him. He turned to the left and felt it on his parched lips. Kortschenko opened his mouth and drank in the sweet snow.

In der Dunkelheit
In der Einsamkeit
In der Traurigkeit

He was surprised not to have realized it before. It was perfectly clear. Everything was perfectly clear.

Für die Ewigkeit
Für die Ewigkeit
Für die Ewigkeit
Für die Ewigkeit

The snow tasted just like the young wine in Grinzing.

ABOUT THE AUTHOR

Alexander J. Motyl is a writer, painter, and professor. He is the author of four novels, *Whiskey Priest*, *Who Killed Andrei Warhol*, *The Jew Who Was Ukrainian*, and *Sweet Snow*, and two novellas, *Flippancy* and *My Orchidia*; his poems have appeared in *Mayday*, *Counterexample Poetics*, *Istanbul Literary Review*, *Orion Headless*, *The Battered Suitcase*, *Red River Review*, *Green Door*, and *New York Quarterly*. He has done performances of his fiction and poetry at the Cornelia Street Café and the Bowery Poetry Club in New York. Motyl's artwork is represented on the Internet gallery, www.artsicle.com, and has been exhibited in solo and group shows in New York, Philadelphia, Westport, and Toronto. He teaches at Rutgers University-Newark and lives in New York.

CPSIA information can be obtained at www.ICGtesting.com
Printed in the USA
BVOW02s1454260813

329394BV00002B/11/P